D1249062

THE
GOLDEN
PHOENIX

AND OTHER FRENCH-CANADIAN FAIRY TALES

By

MARIUS BARBEAU

Retold by

MICHAEL HORNYANSKY

Illustrated by

ARTHUR PRICE

NEW YORK

HENRY Z. WALCK, INC. 1958

THE
GOLDEN
PHOENIX

AND OTHER FRENCH-CANADIAN FAIRY TALES

Printed in Canada by

McCORQUODALE AND BLADES (PRINTERS) LIMITED

C. B

THE
GOLDEN
PHOENIX

There was once a King renowned for his wisdom. And how did he come to be so wise? Well, in his garden there grew a magic tree; and every night that tree bore one silver apple—the apple of wisdom. Each morning the King would take it from the tree and eat it while the trumpets blew. As a result he governed wisely and well, and all his people lived happily.

Then a strange thing happened. One morning, when the King came to pick the apple, it was gone. No one saw it go; and no one admitted to taking it.

"Someone has stolen the silver apple," said the King

7

grimly. The next night he set his royal guards about the tree to keep watch.

But to no avail. In the evening the silver apple was there, ripening on its branch; in the morning it had gone. The guards swore that no one had passed them during the night.

The King called his three sons to him.

"This is a serious matter," he said. "Someone is stealing the silver apple during the night, and not even my royal guards can catch him. My sons, I put the task in your hands. Whichever one of you succeeds in catching the thief will be rewarded with my crown and my kingdom."

"I will stand guard tonight," promised the eldest prince.

That evening he went into the garden and prepared to spend the night at the foot of the tree. He took a bottle of wine to keep himself company. From time to time he poured himself a cupful and gulped it down. Then as midnight drew near, he began to yawn.

"I must not fall asleep," he told himself. And he got up and marched around the tree. He could see the silver apple gleaming in the moonlight.

But soon he was too tired to go on walking. Surely it would do no harm to sit down for a moment? He sat down. Pop! He fell asleep.

When he woke, the damage was done. The silver apple had vanished.

"Well," he said, "good-bye to the crown!"

Next morning the King asked for news of the thief, and of

course there was no news. The eldest prince had gone to sleep at his post.

"Leave it to me, Father," said the second prince. "I'll catch your thief."

The King shook his head doubtfully. But next evening the second prince went into the garden and prepared to spend the night at the foot of the tree. He took a platter of food to keep himself company. He felt sure that cold chicken and potato salad would keep him awake. But as midnight drew near he began to yawn.

"No one is going to bewitch me into falling asleep," he told himself. And he got up and marched around the tree. The apple was still there, gleaming in the moonlight.

But soon he was too tired to go on walking. Surely it would do no harm to sit down for a moment? He sat down. Pop! He fell asleep.

When he woke an hour later he jumped to his feet. But the damage was done. The silver apple had vanished.

"Well, that's that," he said. "I too have lost the crown."

Next morning the King asked if he had had better luck than his brother.

"No, Father," said the second prince, ashamed. "I stayed awake till midnight. But when midnight struck, I was sleeping like a badger."

Petit Jean, the youngest prince, burst out laughing. "A fine pair of sentries you are!"

"It's easy for you to talk," said his brother crossly. "You were sound asleep in your bed."

"All the same, if the King my father sends me to stand guard, *I* will bring back news of how the apple disappears."

"My dear son," said the King. "This is no ordinary thief. How can you be so sure you'll do better than your brothers?"

"Well," said Petit Jean, "I'm sure I can do no worse."

And so next evening he went into the garden and prepared to spend the night there. He looked up at the silver apple, gleaming by the light of the moon. Then he sat down to wait. When he felt himself growing sleepy, he got up and marched around the tree. But as midnight drew near, he began to yawn.

"This will never do," he told himself. "If I fall asleep, the apple will disappear as usual—and how my brothers will laugh!"

He climbed up into the tree and settled himself in a forked branch near the magic fruit. Then he put out his hand to the apple. It was as smooth as ivory, and cool as the night.

"Suppose I picked it now," he thought. "Then no one would be able to steal it without my noticing."

He plucked the apple from the branch and put it inside his shirt. Then he tucked in his shirt and buttoned it right up to the neck. Not a moment too soon. Pop! His eyes closed and he fell sound asleep.

But he was waked almost at once by something pulling

at his shirt. Seeing a bright shadow in front of him, he reached out to grapple with the thief. He hung on with all his strength, but the thief broke free, leaving his hands full of shining feathers.

He felt in his shirt. The apple was gone.

"Oh, well," he said, "at least I have some evidence."

He tucked the feathers in his shirt and went to bed. Next morning, when the King asked for news of the thief, Petit Jean spread the feathers on the table.

"I couldn't hold him," he said. "But he left these behind in my hands."

"A fine thing," sneered his brothers, who were jealous of his success. "To have the thief in your hands and let him go!"

"Hush!" said the King, staring at the bright feathers. "I know this bird—it is the Golden Phoenix. No man can hold him against his will. Petit Jean, do you know in which direction he flew?"

"He left a fiery trail behind him, like a shooting star," said Petit Jean. "I saw him go over the top of the Glass Mountain."

"Good," said the King. "We shall be able to follow his trail."

And they all set off toward the Glass Mountain. Along the path from time to time they found a shining feather. But at the top of the Glass Mountain they stopped. They could see the shining feathers leading down into the Great

Sultan's country. But they could not follow, for on this side
the mountain fell away in a sheer cliff, a thousand feet
straight down.

"We can go no farther," said the King.

"Father, look," said Petit Jean. "I've found a trap-door."

"A trap-door in a mountain?" scoffed his brothers.
"Ridiculous!"

"Please, Father, come and see," repeated Petit Jean.
"Perhaps it leads down into the Great Sultan's country."

The King came over to see the trap-door and decided it
was worth looking into. All of them heaved together, and

at last they managed to pull it open. Underneath they found a well going down into darkness.

"The sides are as smooth as ice," said the elder princes. "There is no way to climb down."

"We need a good long rope," said the King, "and a stout basket on the end of it."

These things were brought from the castle. To the end of the rope the princes tied a basket big enough for a man to sit in. On the King's advice they also attached a string to the basket, fastened at the other end to a bell.

"So if there is danger," he explained, "whoever is in the basket can signal us here at the top. Now, who is going down?"

The eldest prince turned white. "Not I," he said. "I can't stand heights."

The second prince turned green. "Not I," he said. "I don't like the dark."

Petit Jean laughed. "Then it's my adventure," he said. "Wish me luck, Father."

"Good luck, my boy," said the King. "And take with you this sword. Use it well, and it will keep you from harm. We shall keep watch here. When you come back and ring the bell, we will pull you up."

Petit Jean said goodbye and climbed into the basket. Down, down, down he went, with the sword in one hand and the bell-rope in the other. For a long time he heard nothing and saw nothing. Then at last the basket stopped with a bump. He climbed out and gave two quick tugs on the bell-rope. Then he groped his way along a tunnel towards a faint light.

"Just as I thought," he said. "It leads into the Great Sultan's country."

The light grew stronger, and the tunnel widened into a cavern. But here Petit Jean found his way barred. In the middle of the cavern stood a fierce beast with one long horn in the middle of its forehead. When it saw him it bellowed.

"I am the Unicorn of the Cave," it said. "You may not pass!"

"But I must pass," said the prince. "I am on my way to see the Sultan."

"Then prepare for combat!" said the Unicorn.

And without another word it charged at him, the long sharp horn pointing straight at his heart. Petit Jean had no time to use his sword. At the last moment he dodged to one side, and the Unicorn thundered past. There was a terrific crash. The Unicorn had stuck fast in the wall of the cavern.

"Now may I pass?" asked Petit Jean.

"Yes, as far as I'm concerned," grunted the Unicorn as it tried to work its horn free.

But Petit Jean could not pass. This time his way was barred by a great Lion, waving his tail menacingly.

"I am the Lion of the Cave," he roared. "Prepare for combat!"

And without another word he sprang straight at Petit Jean. The prince stood firm, and at the last moment swung his sword. *Snick!* He shaved the whiskers off the Lion's left cheek. With a fierce roar the Lion sprang again. Petit Jean swung his sword on the other side — *snick!* — and shaved the whiskers off the Lion's right cheek.

At this the Lion gave a deafening roar. He gathered himself for one more leap, and came down on Petit Jean with his paws out and his mouth open. This time the prince judged his moment very carefully. *Snick, snack!* And the Lion's head tumbled to the ground.

"Ouch!" said the Lion. Petit Jean was amazed to see him pick up his head with his front paws and set it on his neck again, as good as new.

"Now may I pass?" asked Petit Jean. "Or must I do it again?"

"Oh, no," said the Lion wearily. "Once is enough for me."

But Petit Jean still could not pass. The cavern was suddenly filled with a slithery hissing noise, and he found his way barred by a terrible beast with seven heads.

"I am the Serpent of the Cave," hissed the beast. "Prepare for combat!"

Petit Jean took a deep breath. This one looked very dangerous indeed. But it did not spring at him. It just

16

waited in his path. Wherever he tried to strike with his sword, he found a head snapping at him with fierce jaws and a forked tongue.

Then the young prince had a bright idea. He began running around the Serpent, striking with his sword; and the seven heads began to twist round each other trying to keep up with him. When the seven necks were twisted tight as a rope, he took a wide swing with his sword and—snock!—he cut off all the seven heads at once. There was a roar of applause from the Unicorn and the Lion.

"Now may I pass?" asked Petit Jean again.

"You may pass," sighed the Serpent, trying to find its seven heads and get them back on the right necks.

And so Petit Jean walked out into the realm of the Great Sultan. Just outside the cavern he found a glittering feather, so he knew he was still on the trail of the Golden Phoenix.

Before he had gone very far he was met by the Sultan himself riding on a white elephant. The Sultan had a long black moustache, and he stroked it as he looked down at his visitor.

"Who are you that have passed the Glass Mountain?" he asked. "And what do you seek in my realm?"

"I am the son of your neighbour, the wise King," replied Petit Jean. "And I am looking for a bird that has been raiding our apple tree."

The Sultan nodded thoughtfully. He invited Petit Jean to climb up on to the elephant behind him, and they rode back

17

to the Sultan's palace. All along the road the prince kept his eyes open for the feathers that the Golden Phoenix had dropped in its flight.

When they reached the palace, the Sultan invited Petit Jean to dine with him in the garden. They were joined at table by the Sultan's daughter, who was more beautiful than the moon and stars combined. Petit Jean could hardly take his eyes off her.

They sat down beneath a jasmine tree, and as they began the feast a bird sang above their heads, filling the evening air with beautiful music. Petit Jean caught a glimpse of gold among the leaves.

"May I ask what bird is singing, your highness?" he said.

The Sultan stroked his moustache. "There are many birds in my realm," he said. "This one is probably a nightingale."

Petit Jean thought it was probably something else; but he said no more about it. He complimented the Sultan on the food, which was delicious, and on his daughter, who looked more beautiful every moment.

When they had finished, the Sultan spoke to him again.

"It is the custom of this country," he said, "that every stranger passing through must play a game of hide-and-seek with me. Tomorrow morning it will be your turn. If you should win, you shall have the hand of my daughter in marriage. How does that appeal to you?"

18

"It appeals to me more than anything else in the world," said Petit Jean. "But what if I should lose?"

The Sultan stroked his long black moustache and smiled. "Ah," he said. "Then you will lose the dearest thing you own."

"I see," said Petit Jean. "But I am a stranger here. How can I be expected to play hide-and-seek in a place I do not know?"

The Sultan nodded. "This evening my daughter will show you round the garden. Take care to notice all the places where I might hide, for tomorrow morning you must find me three times. And now I shall wish you good night."

When the Sultan had gone, the Princess began showing Petit Jean round the garden. But she noticed that he was not really paying attention.

"I think you do not wish to win my hand," she said sadly, "for you are not looking at anything I show you."

"Dear Princess," said Petit Jean, "I would much rather look at you."

The Princess could not help smiling. But suddenly she looked so sad that Petit Jean asked her what was the matter.

"I am thinking of what must happen to you tomorrow," she said. "I will tell you the truth: no matter how well you knew this garden, you would not be able to find my father. For he has the power to change his shape so that not even I can recognize him. So you see, nobody can win his game of hide-and-seek."

"Then only luck can save me," said Petit Jean cheerfully. "Well, let us have no more sad talk. Tell me of yourself, Princess, and of the bird that sings over your banquet table."

"The bird?" said the Princess. "Oh, that is the Golden Phoenix. Whoever lives within the sound of its voice will never grow old."

"A very useful bird," said Petit Jean. "And how do you make sure it doesn't fly away?"

The Princess told him that the Phoenix did fly free during the night. But at sunrise he always came back to his golden cage. So whoever owned the cage could be sure of owning the Golden Phoenix.

They walked in the garden, talking of many things, until the moon rose. Then Petit Jean went to bed and slept soundly till morning.

Next day the Sultan was very cheerful, for he expected to win his game of hide-and-seek. He could hardly wait for Petit Jean to finish his breakfast.

"Now here are the rules of the game," he said. "I shall hide three times in the garden, and you must find me. And just to prove I am a fair man, I will offer you three prizes. If you find me once, you shall escape with your life. If you find me twice, you shall have your life and my daughter. If you find me three times, you shall have your life, my daughter, and whatever you choose as a dowry."

"Agreed," said Petit Jean.

The Sultan rushed off to hide, and Petit Jean invited the

Princess to walk in the garden with him. She grew very pale and nervous, because he seemed to be making no effort to find her father.

At the Sultan's fish-pond they stopped and looked down. There were fishes of all colours and sizes swimming in it. Petit Jean looked at them closely and burst out laughing. One of the fishes had a long black moustache.

"Princess," he said, "I should like to borrow a net."

"A net?" said the Princess. "How can you think of fishing at a time like this?"

But she went and found him a net. Petit Jean leaned down and scooped out the fish with the moustache. There was a puff of white smoke, and the fish vanished. In its place was the Sultan, breathing hard.

"Humph!" growled the Sultan, climbing out of the net. "And how did you happen to find me, young man?"

"Beginner's luck," said Petit Jean. "Well, have I earned my life?"

"Yes," said the Sultan angrily. "Do you want to stop there, or go on with the game?"

Petit Jean looked at the Princess. "Oh," he said, "I shall go on."

The Sultan rushed off to hide again. Petit Jean took the Princess's arm and they walked round the garden together. When she asked him where he would look this time, he shook his head.

"I don't know," he said. "I don't think your father will forget about his moustache again."

They looked everywhere, but found nothing that turned out to be the Sultan. At last Petit Jean stopped beside a rose-bush and sighed.

"Well," he said, "if I am never to see you again, I would like to give you something to remember me by."

And he leaned down to pluck the reddest rose on the bush. Pop! The rose disappeared in a puff of red smoke, and in its place stood the Sultan, red with anger.

"Oh!" exclaimed Petit Jean. "I thought you were a rose."

"You are too lucky for words," snarled the Sultan. "Well, you've won your life and my daughter. I suppose you want to stop there?"

"Oh, no," said Petit Jean. "That wouldn't be fair to you. I shall try my luck once more."

And so the Sultan rushed off to hide for the last time. The Princess and Petit Jean went on walking in the garden, wondering where he might be. No matter where they tried, they could not find him.

At last Petit Jean stopped beneath a pear-tree.

"All this exercise is making me hungry," he said. And reaching up, he plucked the ripest, roundest pear he could see.

Bang! There was a puff of black smoke, and in place of the pear stood the Sultan, black with fury.

"Oh," said Petit Jean. "I thought you were a pear."

"You are too lucky to live!" roared the Sultan.

"But I have already won my life," Petit Jean reminded him. "And now I have won my choice of dowry."

The Sultan grumbled, but finally asked what dowry Petit Jean would choose.

"A little thing which you'll hardly miss," said Petit Jean. "I choose the old gold cage which hangs in your daughter's chamber."

The Sultan leaped into the air. "The old gold cage!" he shouted. Then he pretended to be calm. "Oh, you wouldn't want that old thing," he said. "Let me offer you three chests of treasure instead."

"I couldn't possibly take your treasure," said Petit Jean. "The cage is quite enough."

The Sultan turned purple with rage. But at last he agreed that Petit Jean had won the cage fair and square. He even promised to give them an escort as far as the Glass Mountain next day.

Meanwhile there was a banquet to celebrate Petit Jean's success, and above their heads the Golden Phoenix sang in the jasmine tree. But all through the meal the Sultan kept pulling his moustache and glancing angrily at Petit Jean. It was easy to see that he was not at all happy.

The Princess noticed her father's mood, and as she had by now fallen in love with Petit Jean, she felt nervous. When they were alone together she told him her fears.

"I do not believe my father will keep his word," she said.

"He is so angry at losing the Golden Phoenix that he will try to kill you while you sleep."

"Then we had better leave during the night," said Petit Jean.

The Princess agreed. "Bring two horses from the stable, and muffle their hooves," she said. "Meanwhile I will fetch my travelling cloak and the golden cage."

Petit Jean tiptoed to the stable and chose two horses. He tied pieces of blanket around their hooves and led them back to the kitchen door. There he met the Princess, wearing her cloak and carrying the cage.

"My father is suspicious," she said. "But as long as he hears voices talking he will not stir from his room."

She put two beans into a frying-pan on the stove. As soon as they felt the heat the beans began to croak. One of them said "Nevertheless" in a high voice; the other said "Notwithstanding" in a deep voice. When they were both croaking they sounded just like a man and woman talking together.

Petit Jean and the Princess mounted their horses and rode softly away, carrying the golden cage, while upstairs the Sultan listened to the conversation in the kitchen. He had a sleepless night, for the two beans went on saying "Nevertheless—notwithstanding" until morning. And by the time he found out what had happened, Petit Jean and the Princess had reached the Glass Mountain.

The Unicorn, the Lion, and the Serpent were there in

the cavern, but they did not bar the way. Petit Jean placed his Princess in the basket and pulled on the bell-rope. His father and brothers were waiting at the top, and when they heard the bell they pulled the basket up the well.

They were astonished to see the Princess. The two princes would have stopped and gazed at her, but she told them to let down the basket again before it was too late. Presently they pulled up Petit Jean with the golden cage in his arms.

"Welcome home, my boy," said the King. "And welcome to your lady, too. But where is the bird you set off to find? This cage is empty."

Petit Jean pointed to the Great Sultan's country, and they saw a dazzling radiance moving toward them through the sky, with a beating of golden wings: for it was near daybreak, and the Phoenix was looking for his cage. And after him on the road below came the Sultan himself, riding his white elephant and shaking his fist at the sky.

The three princes rolled a big stone over the trap-door so that the Sultan could never follow them. Then, with the Golden Phoenix safe in his cage, they set off homewards.

Petit Jean and his Princess were married, and the King gave them his crown and kingdom as he had promised. And with the Golden Phoenix singing every night in the tree where the silver apple of wisdom grew, they lived wisely and happily ever afterwards.

THE
PRINCESS
OF TOMBOSO

There was once a king who had three sons. They did none of the things that princes are supposed to do, but stayed at home all day and ate their father out of house and home. When the old king lay dying, he called them to his bedside and said:

"My children, I have only one thing left to give you when I die. It is an old bowl. When you have buried me, go to the barn and you will find it behind the door. Pick it up and shake it, each of you in turn. Whatever falls out of it is your inheritance."

Then the old man breathed his last.

It was the custom in those days to keep the dead lying in state for a day and a night; but the king's sons were so anxious to see what the bowl held that they buried their father without delay. Then they ran to the barn and looked behind the door. Sure enough, the bowl was there.

The eldest son picked it up and shook it well. Presto! A silk purse fell into the air. Written on it in letters of gold were these words:

EVERY TIME I OPEN WIDE
A HUNDRED FLORINS ARE INSIDE.

He opened the purse wide, and—*cling, clang!*—a hundred shining florins tumbled to the ground. He closed the purse, opened it wide again, and found it still full to the brim.

"It works!" he exclaimed. "I'm rich!"

The second brother was growing impatient.

"Now it's my turn," he said.

He took the bowl, held it over his head, and shook it. This time a silver bugle fell out. Written on it in letters of gold were these words:

BLOW ONE END, AND YOUR TROOPS APPEAR;
THE OTHER, AND THE FIELD IS CLEAR.

The second prince lost no time. Putting the bugle to his lips, he blew a short blast. *Ta-rraa!* There in the field behind the barn stood an army of ten thousand soldiers waiting for his command.

Then he put the wide end of the bugle to his lips and blew again. Presto! In a twinkling the field was empty.

"It works!" he exclaimed. "I'm powerful!"

"Now it's my turn," said the youngest brother, whose name was Jacques.

He took the bowl and shook it. A leather belt fell out. Written on it in letters of gold were these words:

PUT ME ON AND TELL ME WHERE:
QUICK AS LIGHTNING YOU'LL BE THERE.

Jacques lost no time. Clasping the belt around his waist, he wished himself into the castle. *Whoosh!*—and there he stood inside the castle. He wished himself back into the barn. *Whoosh!* There he was back again.

"Well, it works," he said. "Now I can travel cheap."

"And just where do you propose to go?" asked his eldest brother.

"To Tomboso," said Jacques promptly. "With my belt it will be a simple thing to visit the Princess."

His brothers looked jealous. They had heard of the Princess of Tomboso, who was as beautiful as the moon. But they had never seen her, and they didn't have a magic belt.

"You'd better look out," they told him. "She'll play some trick on you."

"Oh, no fear of that."

"Anyway, the royal guards won't even let you into the castle."

28

"The guards won't trouble me," said Jacques. "I'll just wish myself into the Princess's chamber, and *whoosh!* I'll be there. Farewell, my brothers."

Clasping the belt around him, he made his wish. *Whoosh!* There he stood, in the finest room he had ever seen. And sitting on a velvet cushion by the window, eating a red apple, was the Princess of Tomboso, as beautiful as the moon.

When the Princess saw a man in her room, she gave a faint scream.

"Fair Princess," Jacques began, "do not be alarmed."

But it was too late. The Princess had fainted. Jacques sprang forward and caught her in his arms. He gazed at her in admiration. Never in his life had he seen such a lovely creature.

Presently the Princess opened her eyes.

"Are you a man from this world," she asked, "or an angel from heaven?"

"Princess, I'm a real man."

She sat up. "Then how did you arrive in my chamber? The doors are guarded, and the windows are high above the ground."

Jacques smiled modestly. "Ah, Princess, for me it was very simple. Do you see this belt I'm wearing? Well, it's no ordinary belt. I wished myself into your chamber, and *whoosh!* it brought me here."

29

"A magic belt? That's quite impossible," declared the Princess. "I don't believe you."

"Sweet Princess, you have something to learn. Watch me."

He wished himself down into the castle courtyard. *Whoosh!* There he was. The Princess stared down at him from her window. Then he wished himself back into her room and landed at the foot of the bed. The Princess was struck dumb with amazement.

"There," he said. "Now do you believe me?"

"What is your name?" asked the Princess.

"They call me Jacques."

"Well, Jacques, I think you are the most outrageous liar I've ever met."

"Princess, I have told you the plain truth."

She bit her lip in thought. "Perhaps it is true for you," she said. "But would it work for me too?"

"Certainly," said Jacques.

"Prove it, then. Let me see this marvellous belt of yours."

Jacques took off the belt and showed it to her. She read the words written in letters of gold: *"Put me on and tell me where: quick as lightning you'll be there.* Oh, Jacques!" she cried. "Lend it to me!"

"That I cannot do," he said firmly.

"Dear Jacques! *Please.*" And she held her arms out to him imploringly.

She looked so beautiful standing there before him that

30

Jacques forgot his brothers' warning. He gave her the belt and watched her clasp it around her tiny waist.

"Now," she said, "I wish to be in my father's office."

Whoosh!—and there she stood, in her father's office. The king was startled, but she gave him no explanation.

"Father!" she cried. "There is a rascal in my chamber!"

At once the king sent his guard of honour to her room. Forty soldiers seized hold of Jacques and gave him a thorough beating. When he seemed half dead, they opened a window and threw him out of the castle.

Poor Jacques landed in the ditch by the roadside and lay there unconscious for three days and nights. When at last he came to his senses, he thought:

"I cannot go home now. When my brothers hear what has happened, they will finish me off."

But he had eaten nothing for days. He was starving.

"Ah, well," he said. "If I'm going to die, I might as well die at home."

When his brothers saw him stumbling up the path that evening, they knew that something must have happened to his belt. They came out of the castle shaking their fists, warning him what to expect if he came near.

But Jacques was too exhausted to care. He plodded into the castle while his brothers heaped reproaches and ridicule on his head.

"We ought to lock you up for the rest of your life," they said. "You can't be trusted on your own. Get in there

31

under the stairs. We won't have anything more to do with you!"

For a whole month they kept him there, giving him nothing but bread and water. But one day Jacques said to his eldest brother:

"If you would lend me your purse, I could go and buy back my belt."

His brother sneered. "Do you think I would trust you with my purse after what happened to your belt?"

"But listen to my plan," said Jacques eagerly. "I'll go back to Tomboso and ask to speak to the Princess. When she asks what I want, I'll tell her the truth—that I want to buy back my belt. If she says I cannot pay for it, I shall open the purse wide and send a hundred florins rolling on the floor, *cling, clang!* If she wants more, I can fill her whole room with florins, right up to the ceiling. It won't cost you anything, for the purse is never empty. In the end I'll get my belt back."

His brother grumbled, but finally he agreed.

"But I warn you," he said, "if you come back without the purse, don't expect any mercy from me."

"No fear of that," said Jacques confidently.

And so he took the purse and made his way back to Tomboso. He asked to see the Princess. When she heard who it was, she had him shown up to her room. He found her eating a red apple and smiling.

32

"Why, hello, Jacques! And what can I do for you this fine day?"

"Fair Princess, I have come to buy back my belt."

"Your belt?" The Princess pretended not to understand. "My dear Jacques, what belt are you talking about?"

"Princess, I'll pay you a good price for it."

She laughed. "A young lad like you couldn't possibly afford to buy a valuable belt."

"I can fill this room with pieces of gold," said Jacques.

"How you boast, Jacques! Why, even my father the king hasn't enough gold florins to fill this room."

"I can fill it to the ceiling," said Jacques. "For me it's no trick at all."

The Princess shook her head. "Ah, Jacques, you never change. One simply can't believe a word you say."

"Very well, you shall see," said Jacques. "I have a little silk purse in my pocket. Open it wide, and a hundred florins tumble out. Open it wide again, and there are a hundred more."

He took the purse from his pocket and opened it wide, and—*cling, clang!*—a hundred shining florins fell to the floor. The Princess stared at them with round eyes.

"There," he said. "Now do you believe me?"

"Ah," she breathed. "With a purse like that, you can buy back any belt you like. But how can I be sure it will go on giving florins?"

"Look," said Jacques, "it's still full."

And—*cling, clang!*—he spilled another hundred gold pieces on the floor.

"Oh!" said the Princess. "Would it do that for me, too?"

"Certainly."

"Please let me try!"

"That I cannot do," said Jacques firmly.

"Dear Jacques! *Please.*" And she held out her arms as if to embrace him. She looked so beautiful that he forgot his resolutions and gave her the purse.

But she was still wearing the magic belt. At once she wished herself into her father's office. *Whoosh!*

The king looked up from his desk. "Terrible draught in here," he said. "Oh, it's you, my dear. What's the matter now?"

"Quick, Father! That rascal has come back to insult me."

The king's soldiers rushed to her room, captured Jacques, beat him nearly to death, and flung him out of the window.

For five days and nights he lay in the ditch unconscious. Finally he awoke and groaned.

"This time it's all over," he thought. "If I go back home, my brothers will finish me off for certain."

But he was so hungry that he had no choice. Once again he trudged wearily home.

His brothers had been searching for him for days. When they saw him approach, bruised and mud-stained, a pitiful sight, they guessed what had happened. They shook their sticks in the air, warning him what to expect if he came

34

nearer. But poor Jacques didn't care. He stumbled into the castle and his brothers gave him another beating. Then they shut him up under the stairs with a jug of water and a bone to gnaw.

"That's all you'll get from us," they said. "When you finish that, there won't be any more."

For a whole month he stayed there, growing thinner and thinner. Then one day he spoke to his second brother, the one who had the silver bugle.

"If you lend it to me," said Jacques, "I'll go and get back the belt and the purse."

His brother sneered. "Do you think I would trust my bugle to a nitwit like you? You would only let it be stolen too."

"But I have a better plan. This time I won't even go to the Princess's room, so she won't have a chance to steal the bugle. I'll wait at the city gates until the king and the Princess drive out in their royal carriage. Then I'll seize the bridle, stop the horses, and command the Princess to return the belt and the purse, or else I'll besiege the city with my army and put the whole population to the sword."

His brother grumbled but finally agreed.

And so with the bugle under his arm Jacques once more took the road to Tomboso. By next morning he was ready, standing at the gates of the city. When the royal carriage came into sight, he blew the silver bugle. *Ta-rraa!* There stood an army of ten thousand men.

"General, we await your orders."

"Men," said Jacques, "surround the city."

The king of Tomboso was astonished to see so many soldiers, and the Princess was so frightened that she dropped the red apple she was eating. But when she saw who ran forward to hold the bridle of the horses, she smiled.

"So it's you again, Jacques! And what are you up to this time?"

"Fair Princess," said Jacques sternly, "if you do not return my belongings, I will give orders to sack the town."

"Good heavens!" cried the Princess. "This sounds serious. Of course I'll give everything back to you. I wasn't going to keep them anyway. But tell me first, brave general, where did you enlist this great army?"

"Fair lady, to raise an army like this is a very simple thing for me."

"A simple thing?" said the Princess. "Really, I can't believe that."

"Very well," said Jacques, "I'll tell you how it's done. Do you see this silver bugle? If I blow it at one end, ten thousand soldiers appear. Blow the other end, and they all vanish."

The Princess laughed. "A bugle does all that? Really, Jacques, I think you must be the prince of liars."

"You shall see," said Jacques.

He blew the bugle at the wide end. Presto! In a twinkling

36

the field was empty. Then he blew the other end and the whole army reappeared, ready to attack the town.

"Stop, stop!" cried the Princess. "I shall give you back what you asked for. But tell me, does the bugle obey you alone?"

"Why, no," said Jacques. "It obeys whoever blows it."

She unclasped the belt from her waist and pulled out the purse. But before handing them over to him, she said:

"What a wonderful bugle! May I try blowing it, just once?"

Jacques hesitated.

The Princess gave him an enchanting smile. "Dear Jacques," she said. *"Please."*

"Can I trust you this time?" he demanded.

"I give you my word," said the Princess. "The word of Tomboso. If the bugle obeys me too, I shall return your belt and your purse."

And so poor Jacques forgot his promise and gave her the bugle. As soon as she had it she blew into the wide end. Presto! In a twinkling Jacques's army vanished. Then she blew at the other end. *Ta-rraa!* A new army appeared.

"Princess, we await your orders."

"Take this scoundrel," said the Princess, "and march over his body till he is seven times dead."

Two soldiers held Jacques down. Then the whole army marched over him until he was pounded flat into the ground.

For seven days and seven nights Jacques lay there without

moving. But he must have had at least seven lives, for at last one morning he woke.

"This really is the end," he groaned. "I can never go home now."

Slowly he pulled himself out of the ground. His legs were so weak that he could hardly stand. Falling every few yards, he staggered away from Tomboso, following a little footpath that wound into the woods. He came to a marsh full of big green rushes, and there he lost the path. Several times he nearly drowned. Finally he fell exhausted in the hot sunshine at the edge of a clearing.

"Well," he thought, "I'll try to reach that apple tree. At least I'll be able to die in the shade."

Dragging himself along the ground, he got as far as the apple tree. Its branches were so laden with ripe shining fruit that they bent down within his reach. Nearby there was another tree, weighed down with plums.

"It must be an old orchard," said Jacques to himself. "I don't think I'll die just yet—not until I've had a little refreshment."

He ate one apple and a strange thing happened. His nose began to feel heavy, as if it was ready to drop off. He ate another, and his head began to bend forward with the weight. He ate a third apple, and by this time his nose had grown so long that it touched the ground.

"Thunderation!" cried Jacques. "Am I going to die with a nose like an elephant?"

38

He crawled on all fours to the plum tree. His nose was so heavy that he could not stand up. Rolling on his back, he kicked at the lowest branch. Plums fell all around him.

"Well," he thought, "they can't be any worse."

He ate one. It tasted sweet and juicy, and he felt better immediately. He ate another. Better still—now he could lift his head. At each mouthful he felt his nose shrinking, until by the time he had eaten three plums it was the finest nose you have ever seen.

"Let me see now. Eat apples, and your nose grows. Eat plums, and it shrinks. And I know someone who is very fond of fruit. Oho! My affairs are mending!"

Cheerfully he made his way back to the marsh where he cut down some rushes and plaited himself two baskets. The first he filled with apples, the second with plums. Then he set out towards Tomboso again.

In front of the castle he walked up and down, shouting like a pedlar:

"Apples for sale! Fresh apples!"

The Princess, who was very fond of apples, sent a servant downstairs to buy some. When she saw how delicious the fruit looked, she didn't worry about spoiling her dinner but began eating right away. She soon felt strange. She tried to stand up and fell forward on her face. Horrified, she stood up again and began running towards her bed. This time she tripped over her nose!

Feeling very sick indeed, she took to her bed and sent for

the doctor. When he arrived she hid her face in the pillows so that he wouldn't see her nose. He felt her pulse and shook his head.

"Your highness," he said, "this is an odd kind of illness. You have no sign of a fever and your pulse is normal. Let me see your tongue."

The Princess shrieked so loudly that her servants came running.

"This doctor has insulted me!"

They threw the doctor out.

Jacques, who was waiting outside, said: "Good doctor, I think I can cure her. Be kind enough to lend me your cloak and your square cap. I will pay you well."

"No need to pay me," panted the doctor. "I've had enough of Tomboso." And flinging his cloak and cap at Jacques, he ran off.

Jacques picked up his basket of plums, which he had covered with green leaves and hidden by the roadside. Wearing the doctor's cap and gown and a very serious expression, and carrying the basket on his arm, he asked to be admitted to the castle. He was led to the Princess's room.

"It's another doctor," said the maid to the Princess. "This one looks like a medicine man. He's got no little black bag, only a basket of herbs."

"Show him in."

Jacques entered. He could not see the Princess's face, for she kept it hidden among her pillows.

"Your highness," he said, "how can I find out what is wrong with you if you won't let me see your tongue?"

She raised her head to shout for the servants. But Jacques seized her shoulders and turned her face up.

"Ah," he said. "So that's it! Why, Princess, you have a monster of a nose!"

"He's insulting me!" she shouted.

"Do you want to have me thrown out," asked Jacques, "or do you want to be cured?"

The Princess stopped shrieking. "Oh—can you cure me?"

Jacques took a plum from his basket. "Eat this," he said, "and we shall see."

The Princess ate the plum. Her nose grew a few inches shorter. She began to feel better. "Oh, you are a good doctor! Let me have another one."

"Not just yet." Jacques put down the basket and touched his fingers together. "You have another disease which we must cure first."

The Princess was astonished. "Another disease? What is that?"

"A naughty habit of taking things that don't belong to you."

"Why, Doctor, who could have told you a story like that?"

"Never mind how I know," said Jacques. "It is true, is it not?"

"Well," admitted the Princess, "I do happen to have a small belt here, but it's the merest trifle, hardly worth mentioning."

"Let me have that belt. Otherwise I am afraid I can do nothing for you."

"Certainly not," said the Princess. "I refuse to part with it."

"Very well. In that case I shall leave you here—with your nose." And Jacques picked up his basket, ready to depart.

"Wait, Doctor!" cried the Princess. She unclasped the belt and gave it to him. "Here it is. Now will you cure my nose?"

Jacques clasped the belt securely around his waist. "Your

highness, are you sure there isn't some other trifle that doesn't belong to you?"

"No, nothing else . . . well, only a little purse."

"Let me have that little purse, your highness."

"No. I would rather die than part with it."

"Very well," said Jacques. "If that is your decision, I shall leave you. Good day, Princess."

"Wait," said the Princess. "Here it is." And she gave him the purse. "Now will you cure my nose?"

"Not yet," said Jacques. "I think there is still one thing left."

"Oh, there is only a little bugle that I received from a certain young man. I really don't see what importance it could have."

"Nevertheless you must give it up. I must have the bugle too. Otherwise I cannot cure you completely."

The Princess burst into tears, but finally she had to give up the bugle. Then Jacques gave her plums to eat until her nose shrank. When he stopped, it was a very handsome nose, but it was exactly one foot long.

The Princess protested. "Surely you don't call this a complete cure?"

"It is more than you deserve," said Jacques. Stepping back, he took off his doctor's cap and gown and bowed to her. When she recognized him she gave a little scream.

"Yes," he said, "it is Jacques. You have treated me very badly, Princess."

44

She held out her arms. "Oh, Jacques, forgive me! Come, let me kiss you and make up for everything."

"No, thank you," said Jacques, picking up his basket. "I really don't care to kiss a Princess with a nose like yours. From now on, you know, they will call you the Princess with the Twelve-Inch Nose. Farewell, your highness!"

Since he was now wearing his belt again, he had only to wish himself home, and *whoosh!*—there he was. This time you may be sure that his brothers welcomed him with open arms. They praised his cleverness in recovering the belt and the purse and the bugle, and Jacques for his part resolved that he had learned his lesson. The three of them lived quite happily ever afterwards, and Jacques never went near Tomboso again.

THE
FAIRY
QUITE
CONTRARY

Once very long ago there were two little kingdoms side by side in a far corner of the world. Everyone who lived there was happy and prosperous, for the two kings who ruled those lands gave all their thought to the welfare of their people. Other countries might quarrel and make war, but the two kingdoms stood fast in friendship and peace. If ever one of them was threatened from without, the other rallied to its side and together they drove out the invader.

At the time this story begins, there was great rejoicing in the two kingdoms, for in the realm of King Ogla a prince had been born. In his own land there were festivities and

celebrations a full fortnight long, with bonfires and fireworks and dancing in the streets. And from the neighbouring kingdom came a great train of nobles and courtiers,
with presents and messages from their king. Everyone
wished young Prince Philidor long life and happiness.

Among the guests at King Ogla's court there was a beautiful young fairy named Svelta, who arrived in a chariot
drawn through the air by silver dragonflies. She wished the
young Prince courage, wisdom, and manly beauty. Then
she found the Queen his mother and spoke to her privately.

"My lady," she said, "take this ring, which I call the Ring
of Deliverance. For when I look into the future, I see that
one day danger will threaten your son. This ring cannot
prevent danger, but if the Prince wears it he will come to
no harm. Take it, and keep it safe. Farewell!"

And the fairy Svelta departed as she had come, in her
winged chariot.

But she was not the only fairy at the feast. The last of the
visitors to King Ogla's court was an old, ugly fairy called
Aigruchonne. She lived somewhere in the two kingdoms,
but no one knew exactly where, and no one cared to have
anything to do with her. For Aigruchonne was a contrary
spirit who wished the world ill for no good reason. She was
not the kind of person to be invited to a birthday party,
but she slipped in all the same.

She did not enjoy the celebrations, for she was so miserable herself that she could not bear to see anyone else happy.

47

And when she heard everybody wishing the young Prince a long and happy life, she gnashed her teeth.

"I will have something to say about that," she muttered.

And she went away with her face twisted in anger.

Not long afterwards, another happy event came to pass. In the neighbouring kingdom a princess was born. Once again there were celebrations and rejoicings a full fortnight long, just as there had been at the birth of Prince Philidor. And from Ogla's kingdom came a great train of nobles and courtiers, with presents and good wishes for the young Princess, who was called Irena.

The beautiful fairy Svelta arrived in her chariot drawn by silver dragonflies, and wished the princess beauty and wisdom. Then she looked into the future and made a promise to the child.

"No matter what may happen," she said, "you will always walk with beauty. Wherever you go, fair flowers will bloom and trees will bear ripe fruit."

The ugly fairy Aigruchonne was not invited to the party, but she slipped in all the same. When she saw how gay everyone was, and heard Svelta promise happiness and beauty to the young Princess, her black heart brimmed with spite.

"I will have something to say about that," she muttered.

And she went away with her face twisted in anger.

Now that there was a young Prince in one kingdom and a young Princess in the other, the two lands grew even closer in friendship. People began to say what a fine thing it would be if one day the two young persons should marry and join the two kingdoms into one. And as the years passed, it began to look as if this idea might come true. Prince Philidor grew up to be everything that the beautiful fairy Svelta had promised—brave, handsome, and wise. As for Irena, she was not only lovely to behold, but kind-hearted and good as well.

When they fell in love everybody was pleased. With full hearts their royal parents gave consent to their marriage. Arrangements were made for a magnificent wedding party, with feasting and fireworks and dancing in the streets.

Then disaster fell. On the very day before the wedding, the Prince and Princess vanished.

Search parties went the length and breadth of the two kingdoms, but they came back with sad faces. Prince Philidor had been hunting in the woods near his home when he disappeared. His bow and arrows were found, but of the Prince there was no sign. Princess Irena was last seen picking flowers in the garden behind her home. A gardener working nearby told the King that a cloud had passed over the sun, and when he looked again, the Princess was gone.

Shock and despair spread through the two kingdoms. The joyful preparations for the wedding came to a stop. In castle and cottages everyone fell to weeping.

Needless to say, the ugly fairy Aigruchonne was to blame. She had been biding her time for years, growing more and more sour. When she heard the news of the wedding and saw how excited everybody was, she grew so angry that her face turned purple. She climbed into her black chariot, drawn by four winged cats, and set off like a whirlwind. First she swooped down on Prince Philidor, hunting in the woods. Pointing her staff at him, she spoke a magic spell:

"Plague, murrain, pox:
Prince into fox!"

And instead of Prince Philidor, there stood a little blue fox with sad eyes and a long tail. Aigruchonne pointed into the deepest part of the forest and told him to go. The fox hesitated, but her power was too strong. He slunk away.

Then Aigruchonne climbed into her chariot again and set off for Princess Irena's home. She passed across the sun like a dark cloud. Swooping down into the royal garden, she wrapped Irena in a sheet and bundled her into the chariot. In a twinkling the winged cats took them deep, deep into the forest, where not even hunters came. They landed beside a miserable little hut, surrounded by a hedge of thorns twelve feet high. Aigruchonne raised her staff and said:

"Live ever here alone;
No beauty but your own."

Then she left the Princess to her fate.

But as soon as the ugly fairy had gone, a strange transformation took place. The wretched hut became a snug little cottage, with morning glories climbing round the door. Flowers sprang up and burst into bloom. A dry old cherry tree put out leaves and blossoms and began to bear fruit. And the high thorn hedge turned into a mass of honeysuckle, giving off a delicious perfume. For long ago the fairy Svelta had promised that wherever Irena went, fair flowers would bloom and trees would bear ripe fruit.

The Princess felt a little more cheerful, but not for long. She was still a prisoner. Even though the hedge was honeysuckle instead of thorn, she could not break through or climb over it. And she was sure no one would ever find her here in the middle of the forest.

Then she had a surprise. Near the cherry tree a little blue fox poked his head through the hedge. He looked around cautiously, and squeezed the rest of himself through, tail and all. Then he tiptoed over to the cherry tree and began to eat the ripe fruit.

For a long time Irena kept very still so as not to frighten him away. But she was so happy to see another living creature that she didn't want the fox to leave her before she tried to make friends. And so, with her heart pounding, she began to sing in a soft voice:

> *"Blue fox beneath the wild cherry tree,*
> *Please, won't you stay and visit me?"*

When the fox heard her song, he lifted his head as if he

recognized a familiar voice. Then he leaped joyfully into the air, like a dog seeing its master after a long absence. He bounded over to Irena and let her stroke him. Then he lay down at her feet with his head in her hand.

The Princess stayed there without moving until twilight fell. When the fox showed signs of leaving, she thought her heart would break. But as he went he looked back at her with such pleading eyes that she knew he would return.

Meanwhile the beautiful fairy Svelta had heard the news of the young couple's disappearance. She lost no time in setting out to rescue them. First she visited Philidor's mother the Queen and reminded her of the Ring of Deliverance that she had given him long ago.

"Goodness yes, the ring!" exclaimed the Queen. "No, he wasn't wearing it. In the excitement of the wedding, I forgot all about it. But it's in a safe place. Just a moment and I'll fetch it."

She rushed to her sewing-room and found the ring safe in her box of thimbles.

"Here it is!" she cried. "Thank goodness! Now you need only give it to Philidor and he'll be safe and sound."

Svelta took the ring. "First I must find Philidor," she said.

The Queen looked crestfallen. "I hadn't thought of that," she said. "Oh dear, will I ever see him again?"

Svelta patted her hand and set off in her winged chariot drawn by silver dragonflies. She didn't know where to find Philidor, for even though she was a good fairy, her powers

were no stronger than Aigruchonne's. But she thought that if she went to the place where Philidor's bow and arrows were found, she might be able to trace him from there.

Twilight had fallen when Svelta reached the middle of the forest. She called Philidor's name and rang her silver bells, but without success. By the time night came on she was feeling discouraged. She made herself a bed of thistle-down and decided to wait till morning. Creatures of the wildwood went quietly by, but she did not stir.

In her little cottage Princess Irena was up early the next day, hoping to see her fox again. She ate a breakfast of ripe fruit and sat down to wait. Presently there was a rustling at the hedge and the fox poked his head through. Softly the Princess sang her invitation:

"Blue fox beneath the wild cherry tree,
Please won't you come and visit me?"

And the fox crept through the hedge and came to put his head on her knee. When she fed him cherries from the tree, he took them from her with the gentlest manner in the world.

But this time he did not stay long. Suddenly he raised his head and cocked his ears. Listening carefully, Irena could hear far off a sound like silver bells ringing. The fox grew restless. Finally he kissed her hand, as if to promise that he would come back, and disappeared through the hedge into the forest.

Far away among the trees Svelta stopped ringing her

54

silver bells and waited. When she saw the little blue fox running towards her she laughed.

"Well, your highness," she said, for she saw at a glance that the fox was really Prince Philidor, "this is a pretty pass. I had hoped to save you with the Ring of Deliverance, but you can't very well put the ring on your paw, can you? We shall have to think of something else."

The fox danced around her with a pleading look in his eyes.

"Do you want the Ring anyway?" asked Svelta. "Very well."

And she gave him the Ring. The fox took it gently in his mouth, thanked her with his eyes, and ran off into the forest.

This time Princess Irena did not have to invite him into her garden. He dashed right through the hedge and trotted up to drop the ring in her hand. When she saw what it was, she laughed and wept at the same time, for of course she thought it was an ordinary ring the fox had found somewhere. In a sad voice she sang:

> "Blue fox beneath the wild cherry tree,
> Pray, have you come to marry me?"

At this the fox danced around her as if he had gone wild; then he jumped into her lap and waited expectantly.

"Then I suppose I must put the ring on," said Irena sadly. "For if I spend the rest of my life here in the middle of the forest, I shall certainly never marry anyone else."

She felt like bursting into tears, but she didn't want to cause the fox any distress. So she put on the Ring of Deliverance.

Boom!

A tremendous explosion shattered the air. When Irena opened her eyes, she saw through a cloud of purple that she was home again, in the palace garden. And sitting on her knee, in his own proper shape, was Prince Philidor. He stood up quickly and apologized, but you may be sure she forgave him.

Everyone came running to the garden—first the gardeners, then footmen, stableboys, lackeys, scullions, pages, butlers, chambermaids, and finally the King and Queen. Imagine their surprise when they saw standing before them the Prince and Princess whom they had believed lost forever!

Horses and carriages were sent for, and everyone set off at full gallop for Philidor's home to bring his parents the good news. Here again there was joy and tears. Then it was decided that the wedding had better go on quickly, before Aigruchonne had a chance to upset things again. Everybody got busy. Cooks rushed back to their kitchens, butlers to their pantries, and tailors to their needles. Philidor and Irena were married that very day, and there was cheering and feasting and dancing in the streets.

In the evening there were fireworks. *Bang! Pop! Patter!* went the skyrockets, and they sent down showers of stars

—red, green, and gold. But they were interrupted by something that was not on the program. There was a cry of excitement, and people began pointing towards the northern sky. High above them the guests saw Aigruchonne in her chariot drawn by winged cats. The ugly fairy was so angry to see the merry crowds beneath that she glowed red and purple. Brighter and brighter she grew, until suddenly there was a very loud bang, and Aigruchonne disappeared in a cloud of dust and ashes and a few pieces of fur. She had exploded with rage.

So everyone else lived very cheerfully afterwards, with no Aigruchonne to worry about. And their dreams went on coming true. Philidor and Irena became king and queen, and their two realms were joined into one. Every spring they would make a journey into the forest to visit the place where the little blue fox had found his princess. And when Irena had children of her own, she used to put them to bed with the story of the fox who came to eat cherries. The story always ended with the song she had sung forlornly long ago:

> *"Blue fox beneath the wild cherry tree,*
> *Pray, have you come to marry me?"*

SCURVYHEAD

Once there was an old man whose wife had died. He wanted very much to marry again so that he would have someone to cook his porridge in the morning and fetch his slippers in the evening, but none of the women in the village would have anything to do with him because he never washed his beard. The old man blamed it all on his son, a young boy called Petit Jean. Morning and evening, day after day, he beat Petit Jean like a carpet. You would have wept to see him!

One fine day Petit Jean decided that he had had enough of this. He made up his mind to run away.

He took the high road to the west, and walked and walked until the sun was setting. By this time the road had dwindled to a path, and he didn't know whether to turn back or to go on and see where the path went. It was growing dark, and he was tired and hungry. But if he went back, his father would beat him all the harder. Petit Jean decided to go on.

The path led into the darkest depths of a forest. Petit Jean hurried along, glancing behind him from time to time. At last he came out into a clearing, and here to his surprise he saw two buildings bathed in the rosy light of the sunset: a stable and a tall castle with turrets and battlements.

The nearer he drew to the castle the more dark and gloomy it looked; and there was not a living thing to be seen round about except owls. Petit Jean didn't like the look of it. He would have run away as fast as he could, but when he turned around he couldn't find the path by which he had come. And so, his knees trembling, he climbed the wide stairs of the castle entrance and lifted the great iron knocker on the door.

Clang!

Petit Jean waited. Presently the door creaked open, and an old, old woman looked out at him.

"Hum!" she said. "Where have you come from, my boy? Do you know, you are the first person to knock at my door in a hundred years?"

Petit Jean gulped. "Good mother," he said, "I'm lost. My

father beat me morning and evening, day after day, so I ran away."

"Hum!" said the old woman. "And where are you going?"

"I don't know."

"Hum!" said the old woman again. She looked at him very closely, and he pretended not to be frightened by her beady black eyes.

"Well," she said finally, "how would you like to stay here and work for me?"

"Oh, good mother," said Petit Jean, "that would save my life."

"You won't have any company, except me."

"I don't mind," he said, "as long as you don't beat me."

The old woman promised not to beat him if he did what she told him. She pointed at the stable.

"There you will find my two horses," she said. "One white and one black. Your job will be to take care of them. Now listen. I don't much care for the white horse. Don't feed him well—just a little straw and water. And beat him with all your might; he's a wicked horse. But the black one is different. Feed him morning and evening with hay and oats, and comb and stroke him."

Petit Jean agreed, and the old witch—for that is what she was—seemed content. She took him into the castle kitchen and gave him a big supper. After his day on the road you may be sure he had a fine appetite.

When he had finished, the witch showed him through the castle. They visited the great halls on the ground floor, the gardens, and the bedchambers upstairs. All of them were empty.

At the end of a corridor, the witch stopped and gave him a bunch of keys.

"Make yourself at home," she said. "You may go anywhere you like, except into this one room. Do you understand?"

She pointed at a little door, no higher than Petit Jean. It was locked with a padlock.

"That room is forbidden," she said. "If you disobey me and open it, my little man, you will dearly repent it. Mark my words!"

"Don't worry, good mother," said Petit Jean. "I wouldn't dare."

She patted his head, and told him to go to bed. He curled up in the kitchen, where he slept all night like a log.

In the morning the witch told Petit Jean that she was going away for a week on business. But she didn't take either of the horses. When it was time to leave, she simply gathered her cloak around her, pointed her staff straight up, and vanished in a puff of grey smoke. Petit Jean rubbed his eyes in amazement. She was nowhere to be seen.

But when he began exploring the castle, he soon forgot about her. He had a wonderful time. With his bunch of keys he could go everywhere. He opened one door and found a magnificent room with green walls and emerald windows. He opened another: it was all blue, with windows of sapphire. The third room was pink, with ruby windows. In all his life he had never imagined such luxury. But in all those rich halls and chambers there was not another living soul.

"Now I must do the chores," he told himself.

He went down to the stable, where he heard the sound of neighing. True enough, there were two horses, one white and one black. Remembering what the witch had told him, he gave the white horse straw and water. Then he saw a stick leaning against the stall, and picked it up.

"Please don't beat me!" said the white horse, looking at him gently.

Petit Jean dropped his stick. "You can talk?"

The white horse was surprised. "Why, so I can! I never knew it till now—nobody around to talk to, anyway. Well, it's a lucky thing for both of us that I can."

"But the mistress said you were wicked."

"Ah," nodded the horse. "You can't believe everything *she* says, you know. If you treat me well, I may be able to help you in return. Who knows, I may even be able to save your life. As for the black fellow there, feed him straw and lay the stick on him lustily. It's time he knew what it felt like."

So Petit Jean fed the white horse on hay and oats and gave

him a pail of clear water to drink. But to the black horse he gave only straw and a sound beating. Having been spoiled all his life, the horse was quite astonished at such treatment.

Afterwards Petit Jean went back to the castle for lunch. In the kitchen he found all manner of rare delicacies that he had never tasted before. He ate until he could eat no more; and then he went back to exploring the castle. His keys admitted him to room after room, to splendour after splendour. But despite the wealth and luxury everywhere, Petit Jean felt unhappy. He longed to meet someone he could talk to.

Of course there was always the white horse for company. Every morning and evening Petit Jean went to the stable and fed and combed him, and when he had fed the black horse too and given him a beating, he stayed for a chat. Then he went on with his exploring. By the sixth day he had visited every part of the castle—every part except the little room at the end of the corridor. He stood outside the forbidden door and looked at the padlock.

"I wonder if any of my keys will fit? There must be something interesting in that little room."

He tried the smallest key, and the padlock sprang open. Petit Jean hesitated, remembering the witch's warning.

"But it won't hurt just to have a look," he decided.

And he opened the door.

There was nothing to see—just darkness. The little door seemed to open on a bottomless pit. Right at his feet he could see the rungs of a ladder leading down into the blackness.

"So that's all!" said Petit Jean. "I needn't have bothered." And he locked the door again and went to feed the horses.

But all night long he found himself wondering where the ladder might lead. Perhaps to a dungeon where the witch kept her prisoners? He could hardly sleep for curiosity.

The next morning, without telling the white horse his plans, he went up to the little door again and unlocked it. Carefully, rung by rung, he made his way down the ladder into the darkness. After a while he heard the sound of running water, and presently he saw a bright glow down below him.

Petit Jean was disappointed. "Why, it's only a fountain," he said. "Still, after coming all this way, I might as well have a drink."

He leaned down to the bright water, holding on to the ladder with one hand. But as he bent over, his hair fell over his face and touched the water before he could drink. Suddenly the air seemed brighter. He straightened up in surprise. The brightness came from his hair—it had turned to pure gold!

"No wonder she didn't want me to see this!" he said to himself. "I've always been as poor as salt."

He didn't take a drink, for he saw no point in having a golden tongue. But he dipped a few pennies into the water and they turned into gold pieces. Then he began to worry about what the witch would say if she saw his golden hair. He must go and wash it quickly before she came back.

So he climbed the ladder, locked the little door behind him, and went out to the pump in the courtyard to wash. But it was no use. No matter how hard he scrubbed, his hair still shone pure gold in the sunshine. He would have to go and ask the white horse what to do.

His hair lighted up the stable as soon as he went in.

"Oho!" said the white horse. "I can guess where you've been."

"But how do you know?" asked Petit Jean.

"Well you see, I wasn't always a horse. Once I was a young man too, just like you. But I opened the little door, and when the witch found out she changed me into a horse for punishment."

"But what shall I do?" cried Petit Jean. "She'll be home soon."

"Leave it to me," said the horse. "First, do you see that sheepskin on the shelf? Take a pair of scissors to it and make yourself a wig."

With trembling fingers Petit Jean cut the sheepskin to size and fitted it over his hair. With the wig on he looked like a judge.

"Good," nodded the horse. "But that won't hold her for long. We'll have to plan on a getaway. Put on my saddle and bridle. Give me a good feed of oats and clear water.

65

Then take the comb and that bottle off the shelf and put them in your pocket. They may be useful later."

Petit Jean did as he was told. He fed the white horse, gave him water, saddled and bridled him, and then put the comb and the bottle in his own pocket.

"The next thing you must do," said the white horse, "is to beat the black horse as hard as you can." Petit Jean hesitated. "Go ahead—this is no time to be tender-hearted. Do you want him to catch up with us?"

Petit Jean was so frightened that he didn't ask questions, but beat the black horse with his stick. Then he thought of something.

"But she won't use the black horse," he said. "Why does she need a horse when she can travel in a puff of grey smoke?"

66

"I'm coming to that," said the white horse. "Now take the stick and chop it in half. When you want to escape, cross the two pieces in front of you and say, *'Only by the Road'*. Do you understand? Quickly now. She'll be here any moment."

Petit Jean chopped the stick in half and went out of the

67

stable. Not a moment too soon! A puff of grey smoke exploded in the air, and there was the witch standing on the castle steps looking at him.

"Hello, good mother," said Petit Jean, trembling. "Did you have a good trip?"

"Never mind about my trip," said the witch. "What's the matter with your head?"

He touched his wig. "You mean this? My head felt cold, so I thought I'd better wear a wig."

The witch rushed down the steps. She snatched the wig off his head and his hair shone pure gold in the sunshine.

"Aha! I thought so!" she snarled, throwing the wig back in his face. "So your head felt cold, did it? Well, my little man, I'll soon warm it up for you. You'll feel hot all over by the time I'm finished with you."

And she began rolling up her sleeves.

"Wait!" cried Petit Jean. "Only by the Road!"

With these words, he laid the sticks before him on the ground in the form of a cross, snatched up his wig, and began to run. He heard the witch cry out in anger and come after him on foot. But when he reached the stable door the white horse was waiting for him. Petit Jean leapt into the saddle and off they went.

The witch saddled her black horse and set off after them like a hurricane. But thanks to a week of short rations and regular beatings, the black horse wasn't running as well as usual. It was some time before they came in sight of Petit Jean.

"She's gaining on us!" he cried. "If she catches up, we're done for!"

"Take off my bridle," said the white horse, "and throw it behind you."

Petit Jean took off the bridle and flung it over his shoulder with all his might. In a twinkling it became a whole mountain of bridles blocking the path. The witch and her horse plunged full tilt into them, and the black horse was soon so badly tangled that he could not go on. The witch had to dismount and dig him out.

Petit Jean and his white horse galloped on at full speed. But after a while he looked over his shoulder and saw the witch catching up again, like a thundercloud.

"Throw the comb behind you!" shouted the white horse.

Petit Jean flung the comb down. Presto! It changed into a whole mountain of combs, blocking the path from one edge to the other. Before they could stop themselves, the witch and the black horse were floundering knee-deep, and squealing with pain as the sharp teeth of the combs stuck into them. While they tried to clamber out, Petit Jean and his white horse galloped on at full speed.

But before long, looking over his shoulder, he saw the witch gaining on them once more, like a great black cyclone.

"One more chance!" shouted the white horse. "If this

one fails, we're finished. Wait till she's right behind and then throw the bottle down."

Petit Jean took the bottle from his pocket. When he felt the black horse almost breathing down his neck, he flung it behind him.

In a twinkling a whole mountain of bottles appeared, blocking the path from here to doomsday. The witch spurred her black horse furiously up the slope, but his hooves slipped on the bottles. and together they rolled back to the bottom. She tried again and again, but it was impossible to climb that mountain of rolling bottles—no sooner had they got part way up than the horse slipped, and horse and witch together tumbled down.

Miles ahead of them, the white horse slackened his pace.

"Well, that's that," he said to Petit Jean, puffing hard. "I don't think the witch will trouble us again. Now where shall we go?"

Petit Jean thought for a moment. He didn't want to go home to his father in case it should mean more beatings; and he wanted to leave the witch as far behind him as he could.

"Let's just keep on the way we're going," he said at last.

And so for the rest of the day they travelled on at an easy pace. When the sun began to set they reached a broad river, and on the further bank amid tall trees they saw a fine castle with all its windows alight.

"That's where the King lives," said the white horse, who seemed to know everything.

70

"Oh," said Petit Jean. "Do you think the King could use our services?"

"Kings always need help," said the white horse. "Let's go and ask him. But mind you keep your wig on, and don't expect me to do any talking. A servant with golden hair and a talking horse might make people suspicious."

Petit Jean agreed. So they went down to the broad river and took a ferry-boat across, paying for the trip with one of the golden pennies that had been dipped in the fountain. Then Petit Jean knocked at the castle door. The King was having dinner, but his head gardener received them kindly. He was a tall thin man with a sad-looking moustache.

"Parbleu!" he said. "So you want a job? But tell me, little one, why do you travel wearing a wig?"

Petit Jean thought fast. "I have dandruff," he said, "and when people see my hair they call me Scurvyhead."

"I see," laughed the gardener. "Well, Scurvyhead, we have all the page-boys and kitchen help we need, but I could use an extra gardener."

And that is how Petit Jean got the name Scurvyhead, and how he became under-gardener to the King. He was given a little shed to sleep in, just facing the stables, where they found room for the white horse. He spent his days clipping the hedges, watering the royal petunias, and mowing the lawn (with a herd of goats, for they didn't have lawn-mowers in those times). Every morning as soon as he got up, and

71

every night before he went to bed, he fed and groomed his horse. And all these things he did with his wig on.

When he had worked as a gardener for a month and a day, he had a chance to serve the King in a new and exciting way—but that belongs in the next story.

SIR GOLDENHAIR

All the best kings have three lovely daughters, and this King that I am telling you about was no exception. Each of his daughters seemed fairer than the others, until you saw the youngest: she was as beautiful as a starry night.

This princess used to sit at her chamber window, which looked out over the garden. The new under-gardener soon caught her attention, for there were not many young men around the palace and he was a handsome youth as far as she could see. But there was one thing rather strange about him. No matter where he was, working in the garden or

73

visiting the stables to look after his horse, he always wore an old-fashioned sheepskin wig.

Then, early one morning, she looked out of her window and saw him standing at the door of his hut, washing his face and combing his hair. And his hair seemed to shine like the purest gold! But perhaps it was only the light of the rising sun. The princess decided to investigate.

She took the under-gardener his breakfast on a tray. But when she arrived at the hut, he was wearing the sheepskin wig as usual.

"Tell me," she said, "why do you wear that funny wig?"

Petit Jean bowed politely. "Your highness," he answered, "the fact is, I have dandruff. People call me Scurvyhead, and it annoys me. That is why I wear a wig."

The princess smiled. "I don't believe it," she said. "Why, you are no more scurvy-headed than I am."

But she decided to keep his secret.

Then one day there was terrible news. The neighbouring king declared war and sent his soldiers across the frontier. When Petit Jean went to the stable that morning, he discussed the news with his horse.

"Our King is a brave man," said the white horse. "But his army is too small. He is sure to be defeated. If you ask me, we ought to help him."

Petit Jean was not very big, but he had a stout heart. He agreed, and together they went off to a lonely corner of the

74

garden to practise their skill. Thanks to the good care the boy had given him, the horse was in fine fettle and pranced to and fro with his head and tail held high.

Using a rake instead of a spear, Petit Jean practised charging and making thrusts from the horse's back until the horse thought he was good enough to set off to the wars. But suddenly they were interrupted by a voice saying:

"Parbleu!"

It was the head gardener shaking his head and pulling his moustache.

"And what do you think you're doing, my lad?" he chuckled. "Suppose you leave the war to men who know their trade. Put that horse back where you found him and get back to the flower beds."

Petit Jean hung his head. He took his horse back to the stable and spent the rest of the day clipping the hedges while the head gardener kept a close watch on him.

But early next morning, before dawn, he rose and prepared for battle. First he took off his wig and let his golden hair fall down over his shoulders. Then he put on a suit of gleaming white armour that he found waiting for him in a corner of the stable. The horse, too, was whiter than usual: he glittered like new-fallen snow.

Carrying a white lance, Petit Jean set off at a gallop after the King. They caught up with the army in no time and passed through the ranks like a shining arrow. In front of the King himself they paused, and Petit Jean bowed low in salute. Then without waiting for anyone else they galloped straight on into the midst of the enemy.

When the enemy soldiers saw this shining white knight on his white steed thundering down upon them, they were struck with terror. The mere sight was enough to dazzle their eyes, and not one of them dared to raise a hand to defend himself. Instead they took to their heels and fled.

Petit Jean turned his horse about and returned to the King his master. The soldiers gave a great cheer, for he had won the victory single-handed. "Sir Goldenhair!" they shouted.

Petit Jean stopped in front of the King and again bowed low in salute. Then he galloped away on his white horse so swiftly that no one could catch up with him or see which direction he took. When he got back to the royal castle he took off the white armour, put on his wig, and led his horse back into the stable.

The King rode homeward more slowly, deep in thought.

"Who can he be?" he demanded. "Who is this golden-haired knight? If he had not come to help us, we would have lost the battle. But thanks to him, my army is unharmed and eager to fight."

At the castle gate he met his youngest daughter.

"Tell me, child," he said, "have you noticed a white knight pass this way? A knight with golden hair, the handsomest man you've ever seen?"

The princess tossed her head and smiled.

"I've seen no one more handsome than my little Scurvy-head," she answered.

The King laughed. "You and your little Scurvyhead! Be off with you!"

When the princess saw Petit Jean working in the garden that afternoon, she said nothing. But next morning she rose very early and took him his breakfast. Pausing a moment outside his little hut, she saw a flash of gold through the window.

She knocked at the door. Petit Jean quickly put on his wig and answered.

"I've brought you your breakfast," said the princess. "Have you heard the news? They say the enemy will attack again today. My father and his army are already setting out for the battlefield."

"Indeed?" exclaimed Petit Jean. "But what is that to me, your highness? I'm only a gardener."

The princess smiled and went her way.

When she had gone, Petit Jean hurried to the stable to tell his horse the news.

"We must hurry," said the horse. "Today, red is the colour. Bright red, from top to toe!"

Petit Jean went to the corner of the stable where he found shining red armour awaiting him. He didn't wonder how it came to be there, for by now he was convinced that his horse could do anything he set his mind to. And indeed, when he turned around, the horse too was as red as fire from

78

nose to tail! Petit Jean sprang into the saddle and pulled off his wig so that his golden hair fell down over his shoulders. Then, carrying a red lance, he set off at a gallop towards the battlefield, making sure that neither the princess nor the head gardener saw him go.

When they caught up with the King's army, Petit Jean again paused before his master to bow low in salute. The King and his soldiers were struck with admiration at this splendid sight. But before they could speak a word, the red knight and his horse had galloped like a flaming arrow straight into the midst of the enemy.

The horse made a great leap into the air and came to earth before the enemy king, who was so terrified that he took to his heels at once, shouting to his soldiers to retreat. They hardly needed his advice. Off they fled in a cloud of dust, hotly pursued by Petit Jean, who struck at them with his red lance.

At last he made his way back to the King his master, and once more he bowed low. The soldiers shouted "Sir Goldenhair!" just as they had done the day before, and they threw their caps into the air. This time the King had given orders that the golden-haired knight should not be allowed to escape without a reward. But when the courtiers tried to catch hold of him, the red knight slipped from their grasp and disappeared without a trace.

The King rode homeward that day fuming with curiosity.

At dinner he told the Queen and the princesses what had happened.

"Who can he be?" he demanded. "It was the golden-haired knight again, this time in red armour. He won the battle for us single-handed. But I cannot find out who he is. When we tried to stop him, he slipped through our fingers. Such a handsome youth, and braver than you can imagine!"

"No braver than my little Scurvyhead," said the youngest princess.

"If you don't hold your tongue, child," said the King, "I'll give you the back of my hand."

The princess smiled to herself and said no more.

On the third morning she rose again before dawn and took the little gardener his breakfast. Through the window of his hut she caught a glimpse of gold; but when he answered the door he was wearing the sheepskin wig.

"Have you heard of this knight Sir Goldenhair?" she asked him. "Yesterday he won the battle again, single-handed."

"How should I have heard of him, your highness?" replied Petit Jean. "I am only a common gardener."

The princess smiled. "Well, I hope he will be there to-day. They say the enemy are making ready for their final attack."

She gave him her hand to kiss and went her way. As soon

as she was out of sight Petit Jean hurried to the stable.

"Black is today's colour," said the horse. "Because it will be a black day for the enemy. You'll find your armour in the oat bin as usual."

Soon they were ready. The horse was velvety black from nose to tail, and Petit Jean wore armour as black as midnight. Only his hair floated in the breeze, shining pure gold in the sun. When they caught up with the royal army he paused as usual to salute the King, and there was a cry of admiration at his appearance.

Then the horse made a tremendous leap into the air and the enemy trembled. Down, down they came, like a thunderbolt. Sir Goldenhair's lance ran the enemy king through, and the army scattered in flight, flinging down their weapons. The victory was complete.

"Sir Goldenhair! Prince Goldenhair!" shouted the soldiers as Petit Jean came back to salute the King his master.

"This time I must catch him and find out who he is," cried the King excitedly. "I don't care how it is done."

His barons and lords all pressed forward to catch hold of the black knight. But the horse gathered himself to leap, and Petit Jean sailed over their heads. Then, at the last moment, the King in despair cast his own spear at the black knight. It struck Sir Goldenhair in the thigh and broke off, leaving the point still in his flesh.

Nevertheless the wounded knight galloped off swift as an arrow and vanished over the horizon. When he got home,

Petit Jean dug the spear-point out of his thigh, tied a bandage around his leg, and put on his sheepskin wig again. Then he went back to work in the garden.

The head gardener had been looking for him.

"Parbleu!" he said, pulling his moustache. "Where have you been all day, my lad? Playing at soldier again, I'll wager. And what's the matter with your leg—don't tell me you've been wounded?"

"Oh, it's nothing," said Petit Jean. "I fell on the rake and scratched myself."

The youngest princess, who was watching from her window, also noticed that her little gardener was walking with a limp. But she decided to keep his secret.

Next day the King ordered his heralds to make a proclamation throughout the kingdom. There would be a reward of a thousand florins for any information leading to the discovery of the golden-haired knight who had brought him victory in the war. And whoever could bring back the spear-tip to match the point of the King's broken lance would have a princess for his bride—the choice of his three daughters.

People began to pour in to the castle. There were dandies who had broken the tips off pitchforks and knives, lawyers hopefully carrying pen-nibs, and fine lords who brought the points from their own spears in the hope of winning a princess. The King received each as he deserved and sent them away one after another. There were princes and barons and knaves from all the surrounding country, but not one of them had golden hair, and not one of them had a spear-point that matched the King's lance.

"It's no use," said the King to his daughters after dinner that evening. "I'm afraid you will all have to be old maids. This prince with the golden hair doesn't seem to be interested in claiming his reward."

"Father," said the youngest princess, "does it matter who brings back the spear-point?"

"Matter?" said the King. "Why should it matter? I've given my royal word. Whoever brings it back shall have his choice of bride, and inherit my kingdom besides."

"Even if he should be a gardener?"

"A gardener?" the King repeated. "What's got into the child's head? Yes, even a gardener. But there is no use worrying about that. The only person who could bring me the point of my lance is Prince Goldenhair, and it is quite clear that he has no interest in princesses."

84

The King went away looking gloomy. His two elder daughters looked very sad too. Only the youngest princess smiled, but she decided to keep her secret.

Next morning, when she took Petit Jean his breakfast, she noticed that he was still limping.

"Have you hurt yourself?" she asked gently.

"It's nothing, your highness," he said. "I fell on my rake, and a piece of it broke off in my thigh."

"I hope you haven't lost it," said the princess. "It might bring you luck."

Petit Jean looked at her lovely eyes, and his heart began to beat fast.

"What sort of luck, your highness?"

The princess smiled. She was really astonishingly beautiful. "Well," she said, "my father is still looking for the tip of his lance. Why don't you see if the piece from your rake will do? And you don't need to tell me you are only a common gardener. He is interviewing all kinds of people, princes and gardeners alike."

"Thank you for the advice, your highness," said Petit Jean.

The princess gave him her hand to kiss and went her way. She was watching from her window a little later when he went to the stable to look after his horse.

Petit Jean gave his horse oats and barley to eat, and asked his advice.

"Umm," said the horse, munching his breakfast. "Well,

why not? The princess certainly seems ready to have you. But what about the King?"

"He has given his royal word," said Petit Jean. "I shall go to him just as I am and see if he will accept a gardener as his son-in-law."

"Very well," agreed the horse. "But wear your armour beneath your overalls. Then, when the moment comes, you can prove you are Prince Goldenhair."

"What colour shall I wear today?"

"Oh, white, by all means," said the horse, laughing. "It's the only colour for weddings."

Petit Jean put on his shining white armour and then pulled on his overalls and his sheepskin wig again. The horse wished him luck, and he went to join the long line of princes, lords, and knaves waiting at the front door of the palace. He was the last in line, and he didn't get in to see the King until after lunch-time.

"Why, it's the little gardener!" cried the King in surprise. "And what can I do for you, my boy?"

"Please, your majesty," said Petit Jean. "Does this bit of iron fit your broken spear?"

The King smiled bitterly, and all the court burst out laughing. Imagine! The little gardener actually dreamed of marrying a princess and inheriting the kingdom! It was the last straw. And how funny he looked in his overalls and wig!

"I suppose it's something you found in the garden shed,"

said the King. "However, we might as well have a look at it."

And he took the piece of iron and fitted it to his spear.

He stared at it.

He gasped.

"My people!" he cried. "Gather round! Little Scurvy-head here has found the missing spear-point!"

Everyone was dumbfounded. The princesses came running in, and the cook, and the butler. Faces looked in at the windows—including the head gardener with his moustache.

"*Parbleu!*" he cried.

"Please, your majesty," said Petit Jean humbly. "Does this mean I am to marry one of your daughters?"

The King gave a deep, deep sigh, and the whole court sighed with him—all except the youngest princess.

"It does," said the King regretfully. "I have given my royal word. Anyway, I doubt if we shall ever see Golden-hair again."

The youngest princess smiled.

As Petit Jean came shyly towards her to make her his choice, she reached out and pulled off the sheepskin wig. His hair fell to his shoulders, shining purest gold. Then he slipped off his gardener's overalls and stood before them in his gleaming white armour.

"Prince Goldenhair!" cried the King.

And the people took up the cry, shouting and laughing for joy.

All except the two older princesses. They thought it was very bad-mannered of Goldenhair to choose the youngest. He apologized, saying that he could not very well marry all three of them. But wait—he would ask his best friend for advice.

And off he went to the stable.

When the white horse had heard the problem, he said: "I see. Well, my master, have I served you well?"

"I cannot thank you enough," said Goldenhair.

"Have I earned a reward?" asked the horse.

"Certainly. Ask for anything I own and you shall have it."

"Oh, I don't want anything you own," said the horse. "Just pick up that axe and split me in two. Go on—you promised me a reward."

Sir Goldenhair was horrified. "Never!" he exclaimed. But the horse would not change his mind. So at last Goldenhair picked up the axe and, closing his eyes, brought it down on the white horse's head.

Crash! The white horse split in half, and out stepped a handsome prince only a few years older than Goldenhair. He was the prince who had been changed into a horse by the old witch after he had opened the forbidden door.

"Thank you," he said. "I'm afraid you will have to get a new horse. Now then—let's see these princesses."

The King and all the courtiers were amazed to see two princes walk out of the stable, and even more amazed when

Goldenhair told them the story of the white horse. When the new prince chose the second daughter, everyone was happy—except the eldest princess. She still didn't have a husband.

The King's eye fell upon the head gardener, whose moustache in the excitement was waving like a flag in a high wind.

"I know a prince in disguise when I see one," declared the King. "Step up here, sir, and marry my eldest daughter."

And so they had a triple wedding that day in the garden, and Goldenhair and his princess lived happily ever afterward. So did everyone else, including the eldest princess: for even if the head gardener didn't turn out to be a prince in disguise, he was a fine-looking man once she had shaved off his moustache and cured him of saying *"Parbleu"*.

And besides, he always brought her flowers.

THE
FOUNTAIN
OF YOUTH

There was once a King who had three sons. Their names were Peter, Paul, and Joseph; and they all liked travelling. But the King's travelling days were over. He was growing very old, and little by little he was losing the sight of his eyes. One fine day he called his sons together and asked if any one of them would be willing to do him a service.

"It will be dangerous," he warned them. "It might even cost you your lives. I want you to go to the Crystal Island and bring me back some water from the Fountain of Youth. But alas!—as everyone knows, the Fountain is guarded by three giants. Very few people come back from there alive."

The eldest son, Peter, stepped forward. "I will go, Father," he said.

The King was touched. "You are a good son," he said. "I knew I could count on you. Well, go your way, and good fortune to you!"

Peter packed his bag and boarded a sailing ship. After three months on the high seas he landed at the Crystal Island and set out in search of the magic fountain. All day long he followed a broad white highway without meeting another soul. At evening he came to a pasture where an old woman was tending a flock of sheep. They were such fat tender animals that his mouth watered. He had not eaten all day. He loaded his musket and took aim at one of the sheep.

"Take care, young man!" cried the shepherdess. "These sheep belong to the king of the Crystal Island. I forbid you to harm a single one of them."

Peter paid no attention. He fired his musket, went to pick up the sheep, and began building a fire to roast it.

"So you would not listen to me!" said the old woman. "Very well. You must take the consequences."

She pointed a long finger at him, and *presto!* Prince Peter was changed into a pillar of salt. And there he stayed, right in the middle of the pasture. If he had taken the trouble to look, he would have seen before that around him stood other pillars of salt, weatherbeaten and black with age.

His father the King waited a year and a day, but Peter did

not come home. The King slowly lost hope of seeing him again, and wished he had not sent him on such a dangerous quest.

Then Paul, the second son, stepped forward.

"Never mind, Father," he said. "I can take care of this adventure."

The old King was moved. "My boy," he said, "I would not have asked you. But since you offer to go, I cannot refuse. Go your way, and good fortune to you!"

So Paul packed his bag and went on board a sailing ship. After three months on the high seas he landed at the Crystal Island and set out on the broad white highway. All day long he followed it without meeting another soul. Then at evening he came to the pasture where the old shepherdess tended her flock. At the sight of the sheep he stopped and his mouth watered. What a fine feast he would have! He loaded his musket and took aim.

"Beware, young man!" cried the shepherdess. "These sheep belong to the king of the Crystal Island. If you harm them, you will pay dearly for it."

Paul paid no attention. Bang! went his musket. And he went to pick up the sheep and build himself a fire.

The old woman raised her hand and pointed a long finger at him.

"You were warned!" she said. "Very well. Now you must take the consequences."

And *presto*! Prince Paul was changed into another pillar

of salt, right beside the one that had been his brother Peter. And there he stayed through wind, rain, and sunshine.

The old King waited a year and a day, but Paul did not come home. Finally Prince Joseph, the youngest son, decided that his turn had come.

"Father," he said, "surely something must have happened to my brothers. Please will you let me try? Perhaps I will have better luck."

The old King's eyes filled with tears. "My boy," he said, "do you imagine that you will succeed where your brothers have failed?"

"Well," said Prince Joseph, "at least I can't do any worse."

So he packed his bag and boarded a sailing ship. After three months on the high seas, he landed at the Crystal Island as his brothers had done and made his way along the broad white road. All day long he followed it without meeting another soul or finding anything to eat. Then at evening he came to the pasture where the old shepherdess tended her flock. When he saw the fine fat sheep, he suddenly felt weak with hunger. He loaded his musket and took aim.

"Have a care, young man!" cried the shepherdess. "These sheep belong to the king of the Crystal Island. If you harm them, it will be to your sorrow."

Prince Joseph put down his gun.

"Good mother, forgive me," he said. "I was so hungry that I forgot my manners."

The old woman smiled. And when she smiled she didn't look like a witch at all. "If you are hungry," she said, "perhaps you will not mind sharing my meal. I have some bread and cheese here."

Prince Joseph thanked her and accepted her offer. As he was eating, an idea came to him. He felt sure that his brothers had not listened to the old woman's warning, and that they had paid the consequences. He decided to ask her.

"Yes, they have been punished," she said. "They ignored my warning, so I changed them into pillars of salt—just like many others before them. See, there they are, the two nearest ones."

Prince Joseph looked at them and at the other pillars of salt that were scattered about the pasture, some of them weatherbeaten and black with age.

"Good mother," he said, "will you sell me those two pillars of salt?"

"Sell them to you?" she laughed. "No, I will give them to you because you are a good boy. Of all the people who have come this way in search of the Fountain of Youth, you are the first who has listened to me."

From her cloak she took a little jar and gave it to Prince Joseph. It contained a magic ointment. If he went and rubbed it on the two nearest pillars of salt, he would have his brothers back again.

"But take my advice," said the old woman, "and leave them here a while. If you are going in search of the Fountain, those brothers of yours will only cause you trouble."

Prince Joseph thanked her for the advice and asked if she would direct him to the Fountain.

"Follow this road," said the shepherdess. "First you must cross the Bridge of Razors over the red river. The keeper of the bridge is the old black bear, and he is the only one who can take you across. Exactly at noon, you must jump on his back and say, 'Bear, I dare!' "

"I'll remember," said Prince Joseph, who was always ready to take good advice. "And when I've crossed the bridge, what then?"

"There you will find the giants' castle. The three giants are the guardians of the Fountain, but if you are quick, they will not trouble you. They always sleep for an hour after dinner. Go through the castle and you will find the Fountain of Youth in the garden."

Prince Joseph thanked the old shepherdess, and next morning went on his way. Soon he reached the red river and saw the bridge made of razors set on edge. No human foot could cross it; and the river below was so swift and wide that there was no other way to get across. The prince waited until the sun told him it was noon, then he jumped on the back of the old black bear.

"Bear, I dare!" he cried.

The black bear took him across the Bridge of Razors—for

the bear's paws were broader than any human foot and the thick pads on them were tougher than steel. When Prince Joseph reached the other side he asked the bear to wait. Then he hurried along the road and soon came in sight of the giants' castle. He entered the open door and crept on tiptoe through the castle, looking neither left nor right. At last he found himself in the garden.

There was the Fountain of Youth sparkling in the sun—the falling water made a sound like silver chimes. And lying around it were the three giants, fast asleep after their dinner. The noise of their snoring shook the ground. Very carefully Prince Joseph made his way to the fountain and filled a little red flask with the precious water. Then he tiptoed back past the giants and through the castle again.

But this time he noticed something he had not seen before. On one of the doors inside the castle there were seven gold stars, and beneath them was written: THE PRINCESS OF THE SEVEN SPLENDOURS. Prince Joseph hesitated. What was a princess doing in the giants' castle?

He knocked at the door, but nobody answered. Very softly he opened it and went in. There on a fine white bed lay the Princess, deep in an enchanted sleep. He did not have time to count her splendours, but she was very beautiful. He decided to rescue her.

Looking out of the window, he saw the giants beginning to stir. Quickly he took the sleeping Princess in his arms and ran back towards the Bridge of Razors. The old black bear was waiting. Prince Joseph jumped on his back and cried: "Bear, I dare!"

Meanwhile the giants woke up and began to sniff the air.

"I smell fresh blood!" said the first giant.

"Someone's been at our fountain!" cried the second.

"He's stolen the Princess!" shrieked the third.

In a fury they thundered down the road after Prince Joseph. But when they reached the Bridge of Razors it was too late. The old black bear had taken Joseph and the Princess safely across. And when the bear saw the three giants howling at the other end, he shook his old head: they were far too heavy for him to carry, even one at a time. So no matter how they howled, the giants could not get across the red river.

As soon as she was over the bridge, the Princess awoke from her enchanted sleep; and now Prince Joseph told her everything that had happened.

"First I must rescue my brothers," he said. "Then we shall sail away from this island and you will be free to go home."

"You are very kind, sir," said the Princess. "But I thought that when people rescued princesses, they usually married them. Are you sure you want me to go home?"

Prince Joseph blushed. "Well," he said, "we can come to a decision when we are on board the ship."

They said goodbye to the black bear, and made their way on foot back to the pasture where the pillars of salt stood. The old shepherdess was glad to hear of Prince Joseph's success, and congratulated him on rescuing the Princess as well. But she would not let the Princess walk all the way to the harbour; she had a horse that she would lend her.

"And one last piece of advice," said the old woman. "Do not let your good-for-nothing brothers cheat you out of your success."

Prince Joseph promised to keep his eyes open on the journey home. Then he went to the first two pillars of salt and rubbed them with the magic ointment. Pif! Paf! There stood his brothers Peter and Paul, looking very bad-tempered. But they were too ashamed to say anything.

The Princess mounted the horse which the shepherdess had lent them, and saying goodbye to the old woman, they set off down the broad white highway. When they reached the harbour Prince Joseph fed and watered the horse and sent it home with a purse of gold tucked into the saddle. A sailing ship was just leaving the Crystal Island, and they all went on board.

As soon as the elder brothers were alone together, they began to grumble. They felt sure that Prince Joseph had managed to get a bottle of water from the Fountain of Youth, but he had been very careful not to let them see it. And as if that wasn't enough, he had won himself a princess into the bargain!

"It's not fair," said Peter. "What will our father think of us when we come home empty-handed?"

"Are we going to stand by," asked Paul, "and see young Joseph get all the praise?"

They decided to steal the bottle. But it was not easy. Prince Joseph was always on his guard, and he never seemed to sleep. After a month on the high seas, he was looking very thin and tired indeed.

One evening the brothers spoke to him, full of concern for his health. "Why don't you get some rest?" they asked. "You're completely exhausted. Don't feel worried about anything—we'll keep watch while you sleep."

And to make sure he did sleep, they secretly put poppy seed into his cocoa that night.

Prince Joseph did not really trust them, but he could no longer keep his eyes open. As soon as his head touched the pillow, he sank into a deep, deep slumber. When a storm sprang up he heard nothing. His elder brothers sneaked into his cabin and began searching for the bottle, but he lay in his bed like a log.

Peter and Paul looked everywhere. They felt in Prince Joseph's pockets and under his mattress; finally underneath his pillow they found a little red flask.

"Here it is!" they cried. "And now, goodbye to young Joseph!"

It was midnight. Nobody saw them carry Prince Joseph, still asleep, up on deck and—one, two, three!—swing him over the side into the sea with a splash. They were hundreds of miles from shore and they felt sure they would never see him again.

But Prince Joseph did not drown. As soon as he hit the cold water he woke up with a start and began swimming. He could see nothing in the darkness, but presently his feet got entangled in some kind of net. He felt himself being pulled along. And soon he was being hauled on board a boat in a fishing net with a great number of herring, much to the surprise of the old fisherman who owned the boat.

But of course his brothers did not know this. In the morning they told everyone that Prince Joseph had been swept

overboard during the storm. They pretended to be very sad, and everyone believed them except the Princess. She said nothing but took her first opportunity to search the brothers' cabin. When she found the little red flask there, she knew the truth.

"At least they will not get the credit for what Joseph has done," she told herself.

She poured the water out of the red flask into a bottle of her own. Then she refilled the red flask with salt sea-water and put it back where she had found it.

The brothers did not suspect her. They were too busy

planning what to do when they returned home. They would not give the old King the magic water until he promised to give up the throne and divide his kingdom between them.

The day before they landed, the brothers spoke to the Princess in private. They warned her that she must agree with the story they told the King.

"And when he has divided the kingdom between us," they said, "we will decide which of us is to marry you."

The Princess bowed her head. She was determined to see the brothers get what they deserved, so she agreed to go with them. Besides, she was not sure that they had really seen the last of Prince Joseph.

The moment they landed, the brothers obtained horses and set off at full speed with the Princess toward the royal castle. The old King their father was by now nearly blind. But when he was told who had come home, he wept for joy.

"My boys," he said, "I had given you up for lost. Have you brought me the water from the Fountain of Youth? And who is this lady? And where is my youngest son, Joseph?"

The brothers told him they had brought him a flask of the magic water. They made up a story about how they had taken it from the three giants, and how they had rescued the Princess of the Seven Splendours from the giants' castle. Prince Joseph, they said, had been too young and rash for the adventure: he had been turned into a pillar of salt by a witch and they'd had to rescue him as well. Then, on the voyage home, he had been swept overboard during a storm.

The old King wept again when he heard this. "But I still have two sons left," he said at last. "Come, moisten my eyes with the magic water so that I may see you clearly again."

"Not so fast," said the brothers. "First we must have your royal word that you will give your kingdom to us."

The King peered at them.

"Ah, my boys," he said sadly. "You need not have demanded that of me. I would have done it anyway, for I am old and tired of being king. But if that is how you wish it, very well. I give you my word."

The two princes smiled, and Peter, being the eldest, brought forward the red flask. He opened it, shook a few drops on the trembling old King's eyes, and then rubbed them with a silk handkerchief.

But of course it was not the magic water from the Fountain of Youth; it was the salt water that the Princess had put in its place. When the King felt it stinging his eyes, he shrieked in pain and anger.

"Treachery!" he cried. "Wretched boys, you have deceived me! Are you so eager for my kingdom that you will not even let me live?"

He swung around to face his royal guards. "Seize them," he commanded. "Give them the punishment reserved for traitors. Tie them hand and foot, drag them behind your horses to the seacoast, and cast them into the sea."

"Wait!" shouted Paul. "It's Joseph's fault, not ours! We've not touched the bottle since we took it from his cabin, so *he* must have put the salt water in it."

"Shut up, you fool!" growled his brother Peter.

But the King had become suspicious. "What's this?" he said. "You took the bottle from Joseph's cabin? Was it Joseph who reached the Fountain of Youth, not you? Princess, perhaps you can tell me the truth of it."

"Gladly, your majesty," answered the Princess. And she told him the true story: how Prince Joseph had won the magic water, how he had rescued her from the giants, how he had rescued his brothers from being pillars of salt, and how his brothers had betrayed him on the high seas.

"As for the salt water," she said, "I'm afraid that was my fault. When I found out they had stolen the red flask, I made up my mind that they would not get the credit for Prince Joseph's courage, so I changed the water. Here is the true water from the magic fountain."

And she offered the King her own bottle.

"Keep it, my dear," said the King. "I will not accept it until the day when I can see my loyal son Joseph again. If that day does not come, I shall die blind. Meanwhile, you have proved that these two scoundrels doubly deserve to be punished. Take them, and bind them!"

At once the brothers were tied hand and foot and dragged behind the guardsmen's horses all the way to the seacoast. At the edge of the cliff the guards stopped and cast them—

splish! splosh!—into the sea. For that was how they treated traitors in the King's land.

But the brothers did not drown. In the waters below the cliff an old fisherman and his young helper were trolling for fish with a big net. When they pulled in their net, they saw that they had caught two very strange fish indeed.

"Bless my soul!" cried the old fisherman. "Two young men bound hand and foot!"

But he was even more surprised when he heard what his young helper had to say.

"Master," said the young man, "the time has come to tell you who I am. I, whom you saved from drowning a month ago, am Prince Joseph, the son of your King; and these two are my brothers who threw me overboard. Since they have been cast into the sea like this, it means their treachery has been discovered. I am free to go home."

The old fisherman fell on his knees, but Prince Joseph raised him up again and promised him a reward for his kindness. Then he asked to be put ashore with his brothers.

"And I should like to buy some of your fish," he added. "About a cartload."

"But you are entitled to half of the fish anyway," said the old man. "After all, you helped to catch them."

And so Prince Joseph went ashore with his two brothers and a cartload of fish. He bought a horse and wagon, and the old fisherman helped him to load it with the fish and his two brothers, who were still tied up. Prince Joseph said goodbye and drove off towards the royal palace.

When he reached home he stopped outside the gate and cried: "Fresh fish for sale!"

"Be off!" said the King's guards. "And don't be a nuisance."

But high up in one of the turrets of the castle a window opened and the Princess of the Seven Splendours looked down. When she saw who had arrived she clapped her hands for joy and hurried down to tell the King that there was a very interesting fish-merchant at the gate.

"Fish?" said the King sadly. "Why should I be interested in fish when I have no sons left to inherit my throne?"

"But these are very special fish," said the Princess.

The old King sighed and tottered out to the gate to ask about the special fish. The young man in the wagon picked up two great bundles and tumbled them to the ground. The King had to bend down close before he could see them, but when he did he was astounded.

"Peter and Paul!" he exclaimed. "But I thought they were drowned! And who might you be, young man? I seem to know your voice."

"Don't you recognize me, father?" asked his youngest son, climbing down from the wagon.

"Why, bless me!" cried the King. "Joseph! Is it really you?"

Prince Joseph embraced his father, and then he embraced

106

the Princess too—for he found that he was very glad to see her. The old King was weeping for joy. He was even happy to see his elder sons again, for once he had got over his anger he regretted sending them to their death. He had decided on a better punishment. They would be banished from his kingdom and sent into the wide world to fend for themselves.

"And for a start," said the King, "you can take this wagon full of fish. Joseph won't have any use for it now."

Peter and Paul climbed into the wagon and drove off without a word. Whether they made a success of the fish business, no one knows.

But now the Princess brought forward the magic water, reminding the King of his vow. He accepted it from Prince Joseph's hands and rubbed a few drops on his eyes and on his aching joints. In a moment his eyes were twinkling bright, and he was dancing about like a boy again!

"My true son!" he said, embracing Prince Joseph. "I owe it all to you. Tell me, what can I offer you in return for this priceless gift?"

Prince Joseph knelt before him. "I want only one thing, Father," he said. "Your permission to marry this lady, the Princess of the Seven Splendours."

The King had a good look at the Princess, whom he had not really been able to see before. Then he told Joseph he was a lucky fellow and gave him his permission to marry. When they were married, with a fanfare of silver trumpets and a blaze of coloured lanterns, the King danced more merrily than anyone else at the wedding. And afterwards he gave them his kingdom as a wedding present.

"No, don't thank me," he told them. "I've had enough of being a king. Now I'm going to do something I've always wanted to do—travel! See the world! It's the only life for a young man like me!"

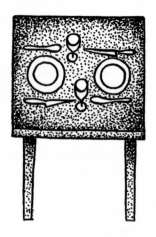

JACQUES
THE WOODCUTTER

This is the story of Jacques Cornaud, who lived at the edge of a forest with his pretty wife Finette.

Jacques was a woodcutter by trade. Each morning he went off into the forest to cut down trees and chop them into firewood. As soon as he left the house, his wife Finette would have a visitor—for she was not only pretty and charming, but a fine cook besides. Not far away lived a good-for-nothing Prince named Bellay, who was extremely fond of eating.

Every day while Jacques was away working in the forest, the Prince would come to the house and sit down to an

109

enormous meal. Finette didn't mind cooking for him. She had no other company during the daytime, and besides, when the Prince had finished his meal he always left a gold piece under the plate.

But Jacques the woodcutter was not so well satisfied. At last he decided to speak to his wife about it.

"Finette," he said, "I have nothing against the Prince, and I don't mind his little visits to our table. But does he have to come so often?"

Finette promised she would speak to the Prince. Next morning Jacques went off to the forest, and soon afterwards Prince Bellay turned up as usual, with a smile on his lips and a flower in his buttonhole.

"And what's on the menu today?" he asked, patting his stomach.

"Savoury dumplings," said Finette. "But I have a message for you. My husband thinks you come to the house too often."

Prince Bellay frowned (thinking was such hard work that it always made him frown). "Too often?" he repeated. "Well, you know, he's right. I'm here every day. No wonder he's annoyed! This will have to stop."

No more gold pieces, thought Finette. What a pity, just when she was beginning to gather together quite a tidy sum! She decided she would try to change Prince Bellay's mind.

"No more onion soup," she said.

The Prince stared at her. "No more onion soup?" he

110

gasped. "Oh, I couldn't bear that. Life without onion soup wouldn't be worth living."

"And for next week," said Finette, "I had planned a meal of roast pigeon. But now we'll have to give up that idea."

"Roast pigeon!" exclaimed the Prince, licking his lips. "But couldn't I sneak in while he's away in the forest without his knowing?"

"He might come back during the day," said Finette. "Imagine how annoyed he would be then."

"You're right," groaned the Prince. "We must think of a plan to keep him away from the house."

When his food was at stake the Prince could think quite fast. After a moment he stopped frowning and smiled.

"I have it!" he said. "This will keep him away for at least two weeks, and by that time I can think of something else. Now listen carefully."

And he told Finette his plan. Thinking of the gold pieces, she listened carefully and promised to do as he told her.

That evening, when she saw Jacques coming home from the forest with his axe on his shoulder, she stuffed a handkerchief into her cheek so that it would look swollen. Then she lay down on her bed and began to moan.

"Oh Jacques, Jacques, I feel so awful!"

The woodcutter put down his axe and hurried to her bedside. "What is it? What's the matter?"

"Toothache," moaned Finette. "The worst I've ever had. Ohhh—I've been in agony ever since you left this morning!"

111

Jacques reached for his coat. "I'll go and fetch the doctor at once."

Finette moaned harder than ever. "No, the doctor can't help me. There is only one thing that will cure this toothache, and that is water from the Fountain of Paris."

"But dear wife," said Jacques, "by the time I go to Paris and back you could be seven times dead with the pain."

"No, no," said Finette, "I'll wait for you. But you must hurry if you are to be back soon. I've made you a sandwich for the road. It's on the kitchen table."

Jacques was tired after a hard day in the woods, but he was so kind-hearted that he left at once and took the high road to Paris. No sooner had he gone than Finette got to work at the stove, and soon afterwards Prince Bellay was sitting down to a delicious supper of roast pigeon and artichokes with pepper sauce.

Meanwhile Jacques had gone only a little way when he met an old man with a big wicker basket on his back. It was the Pedlar who often called at his home.

"Good evening, old friend," said the Pedlar. "And pray, where are you going with such a sad face?"

"To Paris," said Jacques. "My wife Finette is dying of toothache, and I must bring her some water from the Fountain there."

The Pedlar shut one eye and chuckled. "Tut, tut," he said. "Your wife no more has the toothache than I have."

"You don't know Finette," said Jacques indignantly. "If

112

she says she has toothache, then she has. She isn't like other women."

The Pedlar shut his other eye. "And she wants you to go all the way to Paris? Tell me, isn't there some reason why she'd like to have you out of the house?"

The woodcutter thought for a moment. "Well, there's that good-for-nothing Prince with the big appetite. But I can't believe she would send me all the way to Paris just for that."

"Well, old friend," said the Pedlar, opening both his eyes, "never mind about the Fountain of Paris. It just so happens that I have some of its water with me now, so I can save you the trip. Here, you're too tired to stand. Jump into my basket and I'll give you a ride back home."

So Jacques climbed into the Pedlar's basket and rode back home. When they reached the cottage there was a fine smell of cooking in the air. The Pedlar chuckled and knocked on the door.

"Who's there?" cried Finette.

"Only the Pedlar and his basket, good lady. Will you open your door to a tired and hungry man?"

"The Pedlar, at this time of night!" said Finette. "Is a woman never to have any peace?"

Then they heard Prince Bellay's voice from the dining table.

"Let him come in, good Finette. He's an old man, and tired. If you put him in the kitchen with his basket, he won't disturb us."

113

"All right," said Finette. She let in the Pedlar and told him to sit down in the kitchen. The Pedlar thanked her and put his basket next to the stove.

At the dining table the Prince was finishing his roast pigeon. Having eaten so well himself, he felt kindly to the rest of the world.

"Poor old fellow," he said. "He's probably come a long way with nothing to eat. Why don't we ask him in here to sup with us? These travelling men are always good company."

Finette was in good humour again. She invited the Pedlar to come in and share their meal.

"Bless you, good lady," said the Pedlar. "Never turn down an invitation, I always say. But you won't mind if I bring my basket along? It's my living, and I don't like to leave it behind."

"That great big basket in my dining-room?" said Finette. "What an idea!"

"Oh, let him bring it if he must," said the Prince kindly. "He can put it in the corner where it won't trouble anybody."

Finette thought of the gold piece under the plate and decided not to object. So the Pedlar brought in his basket from the kitchen and put it in the corner behind his chair. He sat down to the table, smacking his lips, and soon made short work of the roast pigeon.

"Ah," he said when he had finished. "A fine meal, Hostess! With food like that, I'll wager you keep in good health."

114

"Indeed I do," said Finette. "I haven't had a day's illness in years."

At this there was a strange grumbling noise from the wicker basket in the corner. Finette turned pale, but the Pedlar chuckled in his beard and told her not to be alarmed.

"It's the heat in here," he explained. "Bring an old wicker basket in out of the cold, and you'll hear it grunt and creak like a live thing."

Prince Bellay was feeling cheerful after his meal. "No speeches after dinner here, Master Pedlar," he said. "Instead, let's have a jolly song or two."

"A fine plan!" said the Pedlar. "Nothing would suit me better. But everyone in his place. You're a prince, and the chief guest here. It's proper that you should sing first."

The Prince was pleased, for he liked to think of himself as a gay fellow with a fine voice. He called for wine and sang a little verse that he had just made up:

> *"There is a good woman lives in a wood*
> *(Savoury dumplings and pigeon pie)*
> *Who bakes and fries as a good wife should:*
> *Savoury dumplings and pigeon pie—*
> *If Jacques won't eat them, why can't I?"*

"Bless me, that was well sung," cried the Pedlar, laughing and clapping his hands. "Why shouldn't you, indeed?"

The Prince beamed and called for more wine. "Now it's your turn," he said to Finette.

115

"No, no," said Finette. "Ask the Pedlar. He's a travelling man, and he must know all kinds of songs."

The Pedlar shook his head. "Everyone in his place," he said. "First the Hostess and afterwards the Pedlar."

Finette gave in. And here is the song she sang:

> *"My husband has gone to Paris town*
> *(Savoury dumplings and pigeon pie)*
> *So eat and drink till the moon goes down*
> *(Savoury dumplings and pigeon pie);*
> *He won't be back till the snowflakes fly."*

"Excellent, excellent!" laughed the Pedlar. "Oh, my basket and I haven't had such a good time in a month of Sundays!"

"More wine," said the Prince. "And now, Master Pedlar, will you warble us a tune in your turn?"

"Sir," said the Pedlar, "since there is nobody left but myself and my basket, I am at your service."

And here is the song he sang:

> *"I met a man on the broad highway.*
> *(We travel far, my basket and I.)*
> *The man would go, but I made him stay*
> *(We're full of surprises, my basket and I):*
> *And where he is now, who can say?"*

Finette didn't much like the sound of this song, especially when she heard another grunt from the corner where the basket stood. But Prince Bellay was too full of wine and good food to take any notice. He clapped the Pedlar on the back and shouted with laughter.

"I declare," said the Prince, "you talk about that old basket of yours as if it were alive! If it's as good as you say, why don't you tell it to sing the next song?"

The Pedlar shut one eye and chuckled. "Bless me, why not?" he said. "It doesn't do much singing in the ordinary way—just creaks and groans—but I have a notion it will sing for you."

"We'll make sure of it," laughed the Prince. "Here, basket, have some wine."

And he poured a cup of wine over the basket.

"Enough!" said the Pedlar. "Now, basket of mine, let's hear what kind of voice you have."

The basket creaked, and then in a muffled voice it began to sing. And this was its song:

> *"Good wife, your toothache's cured, I see.*
> *(What was your medicine—pigeon pie?)*
> *The Prince has dined; he'll pay the fee:*
> *For savoury dumplings and pigeon pie*
> *The price is a beating. Fly, Prince, fly!"*

And out of the basket sprang Jacques the woodcutter, shaking his fist. Never in your life did you see a Prince leave a house so fast. He didn't stop running till he was safe in his castle, with the door locked and barred. And he never went near Finette's table again.

As for Finette, she gave up her ideas of becoming rich. Nowadays Jacques Cornaud the woodcutter has onion soup whenever he wants it, and roast pigeon with artichokes on special days. Sometimes the Pedlar calls on them, and he can be sure of a welcome and a fine dinner. While he is at the table his old wicker basket sits quietly in the corner. It creaks a little, but it doesn't say a word.

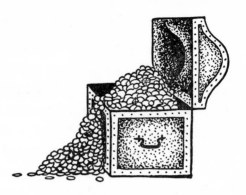

THE
SLY THIEF
OF VALENCIENNES

There was once in the town of Valenciennes a poor stonemason with great ambitions. He wanted to be as rich as
the King, to live in a castle as fine as the royal palace, and
to marry the King's daughter. But as a stonemason he made
only enough money to live on. So he decided to become a
thief.

He turned out to be a very skilful thief. In a few years'
time he was one of the richest men in town, and everyone
spoke of the Sly Thief of Valenciennes. But nobody knew
who he was, for he did all his thieving by night. During the
day he was still a stonemason who seemed to be making a

great success of his trade. He became a master mason, with many stonemasons working for him; and finally an architect, respected by his fellow-citizens. But nobody dreamed that the successful architect was really the Sly Thief of Valenciennes.

Still, he was far from satisfied. He was rich, but not nearly as rich as the King. He had a fine house, but it was nothing like the royal palace. And he had not yet married the King's daughter, or anyone else. So he decided to leave Valenciennes and move to Paris.

Here he continued to lead a double life. By day he was an architect and soon a respected citizen of Paris. But by night he was still the Sly Thief of Valenciennes, making plans for the biggest theft of his career. He had decided that there was a simple way to make his dreams come true. How could he become as rich as the King? Why, by stealing the King's treasure.

He found out that the King kept his treasure in a round stone tower, joined to the royal palace by a stone passage. The only way into the tower was through the palace; the door was kept locked, and the King himself had the only key. And of course no one could get into the palace without being passed by the royal guards.

But the Sly Thief did not give up. He was a mason and an architect, so he knew more about buildings than ordinary people did. He knew that towers like this were often built with a secret entrance: a moving stone near the bottom.

122

So one night he went softly to the tower and tapped it very gently all the way round with a hammer. And finally he found what he was looking for. One of the big stone blocks at the foot of the tower sounded a little different from the others when he tapped it. Very carefully he loosened the mortar around it. Then he pushed gently on one side. The stone block moved.

The Sly Thief smiled. Quietly and softly he went home to fetch the things he would need. When he came back he was wearing old clothes. He had a horse with him, pulling a farmer's cart; and in the cart he brought a pile of empty sacks, a torch, and some mason's tools. He led the horse by a different road so that the royal guards would not see him. When he reached the tower he set to work at once.

He pushed the stone block again and it swung open. Taking his torch and two empty sacks, he crept inside. There was a tunnel, and at the end of it another stone block that swung aside when he pushed it. He lighted his torch. Even though he knew what to expect, he stood amazed at the glitter and the dazzle that sprang to meet his eyes. There were chests full of rare jewels, sapphires and rubies and aquamarines, and others heaped high with gold and silver pieces, all winking and shining in the torchlight.

The Sly Thief wasted no more time looking at them. Working quickly, he filled his two sacks with treasure and dragged them out to the cart. He brought in two more sacks and filled them; then two more, and two more after that.

By the time dawn began to break in the east, the cart was loaded high with bulging sacks of treasure and the stone tower was half empty. The Sly Thief decided he had taken enough. After all, if he had half the King's treasure, he was as rich as the King.

He closed the tunnel behind him and crawled out with his last two sacks and the torch. Then he pushed shut the stone block on the outside and cemented it in place with the mason's tools he had brought. When he had finished, he climbed into the cart and said "Giddap!" to the horse. This time he drove right past the royal guards, nodding at them as he went by. He looked just like a farmer driving into town with a load of potatoes or turnips, so the guards nodded back.

When the King visited his treasure chamber that morning, he nearly had a fit. He rushed out in a fury, then rushed back to lock the door. Then he rushed to the front gate of the palace and shouted at the royal guards for letting a thief into the palace. Of course they swore that no one had come in during the night and that they had heard nothing unusual. The King became more furious still and ordered them to search the city for the thief. Then he stamped indoors to consult his chief ministers.

He had three counsellors—old wise men with long white beards. While they listened to his story, they shook their heads and stroked their beards. Then they went down to the treasure chamber with the King and stroked their beards some more.

"Well?" said the King.

The wise men shook their heads. "Your Majesty," they said, "this is no ordinary thief. You will not catch him by sending your guards to search the city."

"Then how will I catch him?" demanded the King.

They put their heads together, and for a while all you could hear was a noise like bees buzzing. The King danced around them impatiently. At last they came forward.

"Your Majesty," they said, "to catch an unusual thief, you must use unusual methods. We have devised three plans, all of them most unusual. If one of them does not work, another will. Here is the first plan.

"Tonight you must give a great ball and invite all the important people in town. Post your sentries all around the ballroom, and scatter gold pieces over the ballroom floor. When the thief stoops to pick up the gold, the sentries will catch him."

The King frowned. "That's all very well," he said, "but how do you know the thief will come?"

The three wise men stroked their beards and smiled.

"He will come," they said. "All the richest people in town will be here. Do you think he will miss the chance of picking their pockets?"

"Well, it might work," said the King. "Though it's an expensive plan."

He sent out his heralds to proclaim a ball at the royal palace that evening, to which everyone who could afford a ten-florin ticket was invited. The part about the ticket was the King's own idea. He had decided it would do no harm to start filling up the treasure chamber again.

A ball at the royal castle was a rare event, for the King didn't often waste his money entertaining people. Everyone who could scrape ten florins together began to dress for the ball. The Sly Thief of Valenciennes came too. He had a pretty good idea that the ball was some kind of trick, but he was curious to see what the King had up his sleeve. So he told his valet to put out his most magnificent evening dress and ordered his carriage for eight o'clock.

Like everyone else, he noticed the gold pieces scattered over the ballroom floor. But he was not at all surprised to see them; he knew they were a challenge. And he guessed that the sentries posted around the ballroom were not there just for decoration.

When nobody was looking, he took out his knife and slit the sole of his shoe. Then he went to one of the sentries, showed him the shoe, and asked if he might slip out quietly to a shoemaker's and have it mended. The sentry let him pass and thought no more about it.

The Sly Thief made his way to a cobbler he knew, and banged on the door. Finally the cobbler opened his shutters and peered down at him.

126

"We're closed," he said. "Oh, it's you, sir! What do you want at this time of night?"

The Sly Thief showed him the shoe, saying that he had torn it on a nail on his way to the palace. The cobbler came down and looked at it.

"Some nail," he said.

"Like a razor," said the Thief.

"Must have been," said the cobbler. "Well, I'll have to replace the sole. That will take time."

"But I have no time," said the Sly Thief. "I must get back to the royal ball or the King will be insulted. Never mind replacing the sole—just put in a couple of stitches and stick the rest on with tar."

The cobbler agreed. While he was attending to the shoe, the Sly Thief stole some of the tar. Then he paid for the repairs and hurried back to the palace. But before going inside, he took off his shoes and spread the soles with tar. Then he put them on again and went into the ballroom.

All the guests were dancing and casting envious looks at the gold pieces that still glittered on the floor. No one dared stoop to pick them up, for they thought the King had chosen this way to prove how rich he was. But when the Sly Thief joined the dance, he began stepping on the gold pieces: and of course they stuck to the tar on his shoes. Between dances he retired to a dark corner and removed the coins. The sentries could see that the gold pieces were getting fewer and fewer, but they couldn't see how.

By the end of the evening all the gold pieces had vanished. The sentries didn't know what to say. And the three wise men stroked their beards very quickly when they heard what had happened.

"There has never been a thief like this one," they said.

"Idiots!" said the King. "We've tried your first plan and it has lost me more of my treasure."

"Your majesty, we still have two plans. One of them is bound to succeed."

"They had better succeed," growled the King, "for your own sakes."

Next day, following the advice of the three wise men, the King proclaimed another ball, again inviting all who could pay ten florins. The citizens were delighted with the idea, and they came trooping to the palace, the Sly Thief of Valenciennes among them. They danced and had a fine time till past midnight. Then the three wise men spoke softly to the King, who was beginning to yawn.

"Your majesty, it is very late. Your guests cannot go home at this hour through the dark streets. Better to invite them to stay till morning."

"But where can they sleep?" asked the King. "I haven't got rooms enough for all this crowd."

"Don't worry about that," replied the wise men. "They can sleep on the floor. They won't mind."

"Well, there's plenty of room on the floor," agreed the

King. "As long as they keep out of my room. Remember to tell them that."

"More important, we shall tell them to keep out of your daughter's room."

The King looked surprised. "My daughter? What has my daughter got to do with it?"

Stroking their beards, the three wise men told him their plan. The King would invite his guests to sleep where they liked, but they must not on any account insult the Princess by entering her room. The Sly Thief would not be able to resist such a challenge. And the Princess would be ready for him. When he came in, she would paint a cross on his forehead with some special paint that could not be rubbed off. In the morning they would find out who had a cross on his forehead, and so they would catch the Thief.

The Princess was told what to do. She went into her chamber without shutting the door and got into bed. The people who had to sleep on the floor pretended not to watch her, but they could not help noticing how beautiful she was. In the candlelight of her chamber she shone like a star.

The Sly Thief of Valenciennes found himself a comfortable corner opposite her door. But he stayed awake. He was not accustomed to sleeping on the floor—a nice soft bed was much better. He decided to go and ask the Princess to give him her bed.

130

As soon as everyone was asleep, he tiptoed into the Princess's chamber.

"Princess!" he whispered. "Are you awake?"

The Princess sat up. "Yes, I am awake," she said. "And who are you that dare to insult me?"

"Oh, I haven't come to insult you," replied the Thief. "Far from it. I have come to pay you my compliments. In my country everyone talks of your beauty."

The Princess was pleased. "Really? And what is your country?"

"Valenciennes, fair Princess."

"So they talk of my beauty at Valenciennes?" said the Princess. "Come closer. I must give you a kiss for that."

The Thief came closer, and while she kissed him she painted a cross on his forehead. Then she told him to go away before she called her father.

The Sly Thief went back to sleep on the floor after all and dreamed of the Princess. But he woke early, before anyone else was stirring. And when he went to comb his hair at a mirror, he saw the cross painted on his forehead. He tried to rub it off, but in vain. He tried to wash it off, with no better luck.

"So that's it!" he said softly. "Well, this time I'm in a fix."

But he was not called the Sly Thief for nothing. He crept back into the Princess's chamber and found her fast asleep. Beside her bed stood a little pot of blue paint. He took it into the great hall and began painting crosses on the foreheads of the sleeping guests. On some he painted one cross, on others two; and when he came to the King, who was snoring, he painted three crosses.

When the King woke up, some time later, he rubbed his hands cheerfully. This was the morning when he was going to catch the Thief.

"Wake up!" he cried to the sleepers on the floor.

They woke up, rubbing their eyes and stretching.

"Now I want the gentlemen to pass by me in single file," ordered the King. "Never mind about combing your hair."

His guests were puzzled, but they obeyed. The first to pass by was a good old man of sixty-five, whom the King had known for years. He had a cross painted in the middle of his forehead.

"Thunder and lightning!" exclaimed the King. "So you dared to insult my daughter, an old man like you? You ought to be ashamed!"

But the next man had the same mark; and the one after him wore two crosses on his forehead. In fact it seemed that nearly everyone had called on the Princess. When the King caught sight of himself in a mirror and found three crosses on his own forehead, he couldn't get over it. He sent everyone home and went to consult his three wise ministers.

"I must walk in my sleep!" he told them. "Look! I visited my daughter's room three times without knowing it."

The three wise men stroked their beards and shook their heads. They had to admit that their second plan had failed.

132

There had never been such a Thief as this! But they had one more plan left.

"And this is the best of all," they told the King. "Once the Thief steps on our see-saw, we defy him to escape."

"Your see-saw?" repeated the King. "Gentlemen, this is no time for games."

"We are quite serious, your majesty. You must have a cellar dug twelve feet deep under the Princess's room. Then in the floor of the room have your carpenter build a balancing section, like a see-saw, right over the cellar. As soon as the Thief tries to enter the room, he steps on the see-saw, and whizz-bang!—down he goes into the cellar. He'll stay there till you want him."

The King sent for his carpenter and told him what was needed. When the work was finished, no one could see anything unusual about the floor leading into the Princess's chamber. But they tested the see-saw, and it worked perfectly.

"This time," said the King, "the Thief will be caught."

He invited the gentlemen of the city to another reception that evening, at ten florins each. The citizens were beginning to find the King's parties a bit expensive, but no one dared to stay away. They came and sat together drinking wine and telling funny stories until after midnight. Then the King asked them to make themselves comfortable on the floor again till morning rather than disturb the sleeping city at this late hour.

"And in case some of you haven't been warned," he said, pointing to a door, "this is my own room here. I do not wish to be disturbed during the night. And next door is my daughter's chamber. I hope that none of you will be so bold as to insult her."

The guests exclaimed that they would not dream of doing such a thing, and wished the King goodnight. When they were all asleep on the floor, the Sly Thief of Valenciennes stood up.

"Come what may," he said to himself, "I must see the Princess again."

And he tiptoed gently into the Princess's chamber. But it made no difference how quietly he walked. As soon as he put one foot on the see-saw, whizz-bang!—he tumbled head over heels into the cellar. He tried to climb up the walls, but in vain. They were as smooth as glass.

"Well," he said, "this time I'm really stuck!"

But the noise of his fall had awakened the Princess, who began to shout "Stop thief!" at the top of her voice. The guests sleeping in the hall woke up at once and rushed pell-mell to save her from the thief. One after another they ran on to the see-saw, and whizz-bang!—they tumbled head over heels into the cellar. Last of all came the King who completely forgot about his own booby-trap.

The Sly Thief waited till there was a great heap of gentlemen in the cellar, then climbed out over their backs. Several

134

others managed to escape the same way, but most of them had to wait till a ladder was let down to them from above.

"You and your unusual plans!" said the King to the three wise men, who were stroking their beards at a great rate. "We've tried all three of them now, and we're no closer to catching the Thief. You're fired!"

"Father," said the Princess, "I have an idea."

She whispered something in the King's ear. At first he looked astonished, but after a while he smiled and nodded his head.

"Very well," he said. And he ordered his guests to gather in the great hall to hear him speak.

"Gentlemen," he said, "one of you is the Sly Thief of Valenciennes, who has proved himself wiser than my three ministers. I do not know who he is, but I would rather have such a man with me than against me. If he will give himself up now, I will make him my son-in-law."

No one moved.

"I give my royal word," said the King impatiently.

This time forty gentlemen stepped forward, all of them anxious to marry the Princess.

"I see," said the King. "So there are forty Sly Thieves, are there? Well, gentlemen, I must ask you to prove your claims."

Thirty-nine of the gentlemen stepped back again. The one who was left bowed to the King.

"Your majesty," he said, "I am the Sly Thief of Valenciennes."

"Prove it," said the King.

"I am the man who stole half your treasure by way of the turning stone in the wall."

"There is no turning stone," said the King. "I have looked at the tower myself and all the stone blocks are set fast."

And of course he was right, for the Thief had cemented the stone in place when he finished.

"Well then," said the Sly Thief, "I am the man who stole the gold pieces from the ballroom floor by means of the tar on my shoes."

"You do seem to know something about it," admitted the King. "All right, let me see your shoes."

But tonight the Sly Thief was wearing a different pair. He tried again.

"I am the man who entered your daughter's chamber on the second night. For proof, here is the cross on my forehead."

"Indeed," said the King. "And here are three crosses on *my* forehead! You will have to do better than that, sir."

The Sly Thief didn't know what to say. He had covered his traces so well that now it seemed he could not reveal himself even when he wanted to. Finally he turned to the King in despair.

"Ask your daughter to come," he said. "Perhaps she will remember me."

The King sent for the Princess.

136

"Daughter," he said, "do you remember the thief who came into your chamber on the night of the ball?"

"Of course I do," said the Princess. "I remember him very kindly. He may be a thief, but I know that he is a charming gentleman. He came to give me the compliments of Valenciennes."

"Did he indeed!" exclaimed the King. "And who does he think he is, an ambassador? But tell me, would you recognize this thief by daylight?"

"No," said the Princess. "But I would recognize him with my eyes closed, by his voice alone."

The Sly Thief bowed. "Fair Princess," he said, "since I have seen you, I have only one desire. That is to pay you compliments for the rest of my life."

"This is the man!" cried the Princess joyfully.

The King sighed. "Well, Sir Thief," he said, "I ought to punish you, but I have given my word. I declare you a prince of the realm, with a palace of your own to live in; and I give you my daughter's hand in marriage. But in return, you must make a solemn promise never to steal again."

The Sly Thief of Valenciennes kissed the Princess's hand.

"Your majesty," he said to the King, "I had only three ambitions: to be as rich as you, to have a castle as fine as yours, and to marry your daughter. Now that I have achieved these three ambitions, there is no longer any reason for me to be a thief."

And he kept his word. He gave back the treasure he had

stolen from the tower, and from that day forward he never stole again. He did take money from people against their will, and in broad daylight. But princes can do that without breaking the law, and it is not called stealing: it is called taxing.

The King grew proud of his new son-in-law. The Princess was happy with her husband. And the Sly Thief had won everything he wished for, though he found that being a prince was much harder work than he imagined. As for the good citizens of Paris, they no longer had to worry about the Sly Thief stealing from them by night, or the King charging them ten florins for an evening at the palace. So they paid their taxes and lived happily enough.

ABOUT
THE
STORIES

Folklorists have for many years studied the tangled history of the fairy tale and have published heavy tomes on its themes and diffusion. In their learned books a tale bears a number, say 301, and its parts or episodes are given as a, b, c, d, etc., for this analysis is a science. But the scientific approach does not belong here, as the reading is intended only for enjoyment.

Folk tales like 'The Golden Phoenix', 'The Princess of Tomboso', and others here belong to all European nations more or less. Yet in their present form they are French-Canadian from the lower St Lawrence River. They were brought over from France to America by the early colonists three hundred years ago, and are part of the spoken traditions of the country; the other parts consist of legends, folk songs, dances, games, and sayings.

I collected them at first hand from *raconteurs* in the course of many years; in their authentic text they are now filed away in the collections of the National Museum of

140

Canada. They are presented here in a polished retelling by Michael Hornyansky, who is a Canadian Rhodes Scholar like me (but by far my junior). Their treatment in his skilful hands deserves praise, for you must remember that the *habitants* and lumberjacks who used to tell these stories for the entertainment of rustic folk were often crude, though natural, simple, and lively. Mr Hornyansky and I aimed at achieving in our own way a literary uplifting similar to that of Grimm, Andersen, and Perrault in the tales of their people that have now become familiar everywhere.

Out of this selected set of eight stories, two are of a type apart from the rest: a *fabliau* and an episodic story; the other six are fairy tales. The *fabliau*, 'Jacques the Wood-cutter', is an ancient comic narrative enlivened with songs. *Fabliaux* like this were favourites in the twelfth century, and they often went back to the dark ages. (I have read a version of it in Boccaccio, the medieval writer of *novellas* in Italy.) The episodic story, 'The Sly Thief of Valenciennes', may be a good deal older, and it has almost encompassed the world, from its birthplace in Arabia to India and China one way, and the other, westward to Egypt and the Mediterranean. In Egypt it was first recorded in the sixth century before Christ by the Greek chronicler Herodotus, who called it 'The Treasury of King Rhampsinitos'. From China it travelled northward as far as Siberia, and veering westward along the caravan trails, into Slavonic lands, Scandinavia, northeastern France (Valenciennes is

on the borderline between France and Belgium), and
Scotland. It did not stop there, but crossed the Atlantic
into French Canada where we find as many as twelve
versions of it. 'The Sly Thief' is an episodic tale because it
consists of a number of short parts that are almost inter-
changeable in the frame of the whole. This thief is so clever
that he outwits the king and his councillors, until in the end
he is forgiven and marries the king's daughter.

The other stories were also widely travelled, in particular
'The Golden Phoenix', which gives its name to this book.
I first recorded it at Tadoussac on the lower St Lawrence
from Edouard Hovington, an old riverman formerly in
the employ of the Hudson's Bay Company. He called it
'Le Grand Sultan', which shows that its source again lies
in an Arabian country. It must have come there thousands
of years ago from China, because the Phoenix at one time
was one of its four leading deities. The Phoenix was known
as a supernatural bird that periodically dies and is reborn
out of its own ashes.

It would take too long to try and unravel the origins of
each of the fairy tales given here. Most of them are already
known in the written literature of the world. But their
birth does not always go back to Asia. They are at least
in part old European, for instance 'Scurvyhead', 'Sir Goldenhair', 'The Fairy Quite Contrary'.

After these tales landed in America two or three hundred
years ago with the French settlers, they went on being

repeated in hundreds of places to thousands of listeners, almost to this day. We folklorists have already recorded many hundreds from old people, but they are soon to die out because of a changed world. Among the early listeners on this continent were the Indians, who soon took some of them over and modified them in their own way. 'The Princess of Tomboso', for instance, was first recorded in Canada by Paul Radin for the National Museum among the Ojibways of the Great Lakes. And most of the other tribes of the Northeastern Woodlands also made the French repertory their own, sometimes under drastically different shapes.

This type of ancient fiction in which the supernatural predominates belongs to the common stock of mankind. The merit for its immediate expression, however, is not to be overlooked; it must be credited to various nationalities. Here it is French-Canadian. And French-Canadians — through their songs, dances, legends, and tales—have contributed to the enrichment of the New World as a whole, along the St Lawrence valley, in Acadia, around the Great Lakes, on the Red River out west, and in Louisiana. Even the American tall tale of Paul Bunyan of the lumberjacks owes at least some of its features to the familiar stories of Petit Jean or Ti-Jean or Bon-Jean (Bunyan?). Petit Jean is, like Jack in the beanstalk, a puny little fellow, the last-born of a poor family, or a widow's only son, who through his skill soon begins to climb up the ladder, as it were, and finally reaches the top, marries the princess, and inherits the kingdom.

Anyone who happens to require more information about the Canadian sources of these tales may find it in the author's series of twelve booklets, *Les Contes du Grand-père Sept-Heures* (Montreal: Les Editions Chantecler).

MARIUS BARBEAU

OTTAWA,
MARCH 1958

144